A CRIMINAL
CELEBRATION IN
HILLBILLY HOLLOW

BLYTHE BAKER

There's a deadly occasion in Hillbilly Hollow...

It's finally here. The week of Emma and Billy's long-awaited wedding has arrived. There's just one problem: a dead body has turned up and half the wedding party are suspects.

Can Emma use her ghost whispering powers to solve one last crime and still make it to the church in time for her vows? Or will the big day end in tragedy?

1

I was humming to myself as I pulled the truck up outside of Hope Community Church. I got out and looked around at the extensive grounds. The greens of the perfectly manicured lawns shone like emerald and jade. The flower beds bloomed brightly as the sun sparkled down on them.

I knew it was perfect. But perhaps it was a little too perfect. The church itself was a large building, white in color, with picture perfect stained glass windows that glinted in the light. There was no denying the place was beautiful, but it wasn't Mount Olivet. That was the problem.

Billy and I had finally begun planning our wedding in earnest after Billy's workload came back down to normal levels. We worked out every last detail together, basking in the happiness that comes with dreaming of a life together, rather than just a wedding. I was never going to be a bridezilla. I was happy to compromise. Sure, my wedding would be the most special day of my life, but it would be Billy's too, and I wanted his input. There was very little we even had to compromise on. Most times, we both chose the same thing. It was good to know that we were so in tune with each other and that our tastes were so similar.

We had both wanted the ceremony to be held at Mount Olivet, a tiny rustic church with overgrown gardens and large wooden beams across the ceiling. It had been the site of Suzy and Brian's wedding and Billy and I knew it was perfect for our own. I could almost see it lit up, fairy lights strung across the ceiling, flowers adorning the ends of each pew. We had booked it immediately for our June wedding. It had seemed so far away then.

But now, with the event less than a week away, we had learned that there had been a fire at Mount Olivet Church. Which left us without a venue.

Summer Martin, our wedding planner, had called me with the news. Before I could begin to hyperventilate, she told me that she'd already found another venue for us to check out and she gave me the address for Hope Community Church.

Hope Community was brand new, only a couple of months old, and it showed. It was pristine, glowing, but it had no real character. I couldn't help but feel disappointed as I looked at it.

I wished for the hundredth time that day that Billy could be here with me. I wanted us to make the decision together, but there was no way he could get away from work right now. He had obviously booked time off for the rehearsal dinner, the wedding and our honeymoon. He couldn't take today off too, so he had told me to take a look and decide myself and he would be happy with whatever decision I made.

It wasn't like we really had a choice anyway.

I looked at my watch. I was a little bit early, still. I leaned against the hood of the truck, enjoying the warm sun on my face. I didn't have long to wait before a sporty white car pulled up beside my truck and Summer emerged from it.

Summer was a character, to say the least. She was constantly glammed up to the nines, sporting tight little dresses or pencil skirts and blouses. She always wore sky scraper heels and they didn't slow her down in the least. Her blonde hair was always curled to perfection, hanging in romantic looking waves that framed her petite face.

But there was more to her than met the eye. That woman wasn't someone you wanted to get on the wrong side of. She was super organized, and she expected everyone around her to work with the same efficiency she did. She didn't tolerate lateness, mistakes, or the slightest hint of a no. If you wanted something and Summer Martin was your wedding planner, you got it, no questions asked.

I had found her intimidating when I first met her, but Billy convinced me to give her a shot. He reminded me that we were both super busy with work, and I had to help my grandparents a lot more around the farm lately, so we needed the extra pair of hands. I soon realized that Summer only had an attitude with her suppliers and her poor assistant Autumn. When it came to clients, Summer would move mountains to get them the wedding of their dreams.

"Emma, darling, how are you?" Summer enthused as she crossed the gap between us.

She took hold of me by the tops of my arms and air kissed each of my cheeks. Then, she held me out at arm's length and nodded her approval.

"You look wonderful. Radiant. Just like a bride-to-be should look."

I smiled, caught up in her whirlwind of enthusiasm. "I'm good, thanks, Summer. How are you?"

"Perfect, darling, perfect," she said.

She glanced over her shoulder, her smile giving way to a frown. "Autumn? Autumn? What is taking you so long? Get over here right this instant."

She turned back to me and rolled her eyes. "Excuse my assistant. She seems to think you have all day."

I did have all day really, but I refrained from telling Summer that. Instead, I watched as Autumn came over to us, lugging a heavy looking box.

She was the polar opposite to Summer. Her mousey brown hair was frizzy and she always wore it pulled back in a loose ponytail. Straggles hung around her face, frizzing up even more than usual in the heat. Her glasses had slipped down her nose but she didn't have a spare hand to push them back up. Where Summer oozed elegance, Autumn oozed thrift shop in her mismatched outfit of a long, hippy style skirt and a bright purple button-down shirt.

When I first met the two women, I had wondered how they had even met, let alone ended up working together. Summer had told me not long after that Autumn was her sister. I got the impression Summer kept her around because it was expected of her, but I couldn't for the life of me work out why Autumn continued to work for Summer, who was constantly snapping at her and criticizing everything she did. Oh well, there was nothing so strange as family, I guessed.

Summer rolled her eyes again as Autumn finally joined us. "Put the box in the back of Emma's truck. Honestly, Autumn, I don't need you messing this up. *Now*." She barked the last word and snapped her fingers twice.

The longsuffering Autumn didn't respond, she just moved to put the box in the truck.

I gave her a sympathetic look and she grinned at me.

"Those are the sample wedding favors you asked to see," Summer explained to me. "There are a few different varieties. If you can let me know by the end of tomorrow which one you'd like to go with, I'll get that organized for you."

"I can let you know today," I promised her.

There was no way I was making Summer Martin wait. I had come to like her, but I still didn't want to get on the wrong side of her sharp tongue.

She nodded her head and then clapped her hands again, making me jump slightly. If she noticed, she didn't comment. She turned and began to walk away.

"Let's go and see this fantastic venue," she trilled.

Autumn caught up with me and we exchanged an amused look, as Summer marched along giving us a running commentary of the grounds we walked through. She pointed out the various flower beds, and gave her opinion on the best places to have our pictures taken.

"But don't worry too much about that just yet. Derrick Williams is booked and he is the king of location. He'll be along shortly to take a look around and find the best spots," Summer went on.

She paused to check the time on her cell phone.

"Actually, he should be here by now. He might be the king of location, but clearly he's not even a prince of punctuality. Autumn, give him a call and see what's keeping him. And make it clear this is not acceptable."

"He's only a minute late, Summer. Like literally one minute," Autumn said quietly.

Summer stopped walking so abruptly I almost ran into her back. She spun around to face Autumn.

"Is one minute late not still late? Will so much as one minute late cut it for Emma's wedding? Do you think she deserves less than the very best?"

"I ... no, of course not," Autumn stammered, blushing furiously. She turned to face me. "I didn't mean that, Emma. I just ..."

"It's okay," I cut her off, feeling sorry for her. "I know what you meant and it's fine."

"Emma is just being polite," Summer snapped. "It's not fine at all. It's not even close to fine. Now do as I said and call Derrick. Deal with it, Autumn, or do I have to do that myself and leave you completely useless?"

Autumn scuttled away, pulling out a cell phone and scrolling through her contacts.

Summer began walking again and I followed her. I

fell into step beside her, feeling a little uncomfortable about the way she was treating Autumn.

"Emma, you look upset. What is it?" Summer asked as we walked up the winding path to the church's entranceway.

I reminded myself that the relationship between these two women was none of my business, and that if Autumn accepted it the way she did, who was I to tell Summer off for it? Instead, I decided to tell her my other concern, one that was entirely my business.

"I'm sorry," I said. "I just ... I know this place is beautiful, there's no denying that. But, well, it's very different from Mount Olivet, isn't it?"

"It is and I'm sorry about that. But it's the height of the wedding season and all of the rustic places book up months in advance. Even this place, which is so new, was reluctant to see us on such short notice. You have no idea the strings I had to pull to make this happen. But it's your day, darling, and if you hate this site I will find you somewhere else if it kills me. But just take a look, huh? You might fall in love with it."

I nodded. I doubted I'd be falling in love with the church, but Summer was right; I couldn't judge it by the outside. I wanted to go in with an open mind and at least give it a fair look.

We reached the door and Summer stopped and turned to face the grounds, motioning for me to do the same.

I gasped as I turned around. The view was absolutely breathtaking, even though we had only climbed a few feet. The grounds lay in front of us, and through the trees, the town was just in sight. It was like another world, an enchanted forest. It was all set before a backdrop of purple mountains that stretched out as far as the eye could see.

"Imagine coming out of the church as Mrs. Emma Stone. Your friends and family line this path, throwing confetti over you both, laughing and celebrating. The sun is shining, the grounds are beautiful. And you have this view."

I started to imagine it and I could see myself doing just that. Maybe it was a good thing the path here wasn't lined with cobblestones, like at Mount Olivet. After all, my wedding shoes were hardly practical for walking on something bumpy.

Summer turned back to the door and threw it open with a flourish. She led me through a small entryway. The church was all white walls and gold trim. Each window was lined with gold details, and the cross above the altar was bright gold. The pews were polished mahogany, shining and clean. The floor was a stone effect hardwood floor.

Summer began to lead me down the aisle.

"Imagine your flowers here and here," she said, pointing to ends of the pews. "The reds of the roses will look so stunning against the mahogany. The white ones will look delicate, even whiter against the dark wood. And the gold trim gives it such a royal feeling, doesn't it? It'll be like your own princess fairytale wedding."

The more she talked, the more convinced I was becoming that this wasn't such a bad idea. I'd never seen the inside of Hope Community Church before, because Billy and I had immediately ruled it out as too modern when we were looking for a venue. We both enjoyed learning more about Hillbilly Hollow's colorful history and we knew that we wanted somewhere that fit that picture. But there was no denying this place was special.

"Come on, come and see where you'll be exchanging your vows," Summer said.

She was talking like this venue was a done deal, and I supposed it was. I didn't pull her up on her comment, I just followed her. The door to the church opened and closed again and Autumn appeared.

"Did you speak to Derrick?" Summer demanded.

Autumn nodded. "Yes. He was stuck in traffic. He's here now, though."

"Where is he?" Summer demanded.

"He's out front looking for the flowerbed with the best light, and then he's going around back," Autumn said.

Summer nodded and stepped away from me. "Show Emma the altar and answer any questions she might have. I'm going to go and give Derrick a piece of my mind. Meet me around back. And don't give the secret away."

"Secret?" I asked as Autumn nodded meekly.

Summer grinned at me. "You have to see it to appreciate it, Emma, and once you do, you'll fall in love with this place. I just know you will. But to get the full effect of it, it has to be a secret until you can see for yourself."

"Okay." I laughed, once more caught up in her enthusiasm.

Summer walked away and Autumn smiled awkwardly at me. "She can be quite the handful," she said in a conspiratorial whisper. "And I would not like to be Derrick when she catches up to him."

"No, me neither." I laughed again.

Autumn led me further down the aisle towards the altar. She looked to her left and then her right and then she leaned in close to me as if she was expecting Summer to jump out from behind a pew at any second and catch her gossiping.

"You didn't hear this from me but Summer and Derrick used to date, you know. They were together for almost two years and then he dumped her. She claims she's over it but you never can tell with her. The way she treats him, she sure doesn't seem over it. I reckon one day he'll snap. I'm always saying to her, Summer, one day that man is going to conk you over the head with a shovel."

"You really think he'd go that far?" I asked, shocked at her revelation.

She wrinkled her nose. "Well, no, not really. But you never can tell, can you? Anyway, Derrick isn't alone in being treated badly by Summer, is he? I mean, you've heard the way she talks to me and I'm her sister for Heaven's sake."

This was the most I had ever heard Autumn say. She was usually quiet in her sister's presence, speaking only when spoken to. I kind of liked this more outspoken version of her and I decided to try and satisfy my curiosity while she seemed to be in a talking mood.

"Why do you keep working for her if she's always so mean to you?" I asked.

Autumn giggled nervously. "Working for her? That's a

joke," she said. She didn't explain what she meant by that, but left it a mystery.

We reached the altar before I could say anything else and Autumn stepped up a few steps. She disappeared behind a wall for a moment and came back with a decorative metal arch. She placed it in the spot where Billy and I would be standing to exchange our vows.

My curiosity was far from satisfied on the Autumn and Summer front. Autumn's answer just made me more confused, but I didn't like to pry further into the relationship of the sisters.

Autumn said, "This arch will be draped with greenery and cherry blossoms. Some large feature flowers that match your bouquet will be scattered through it. Can you imagine anything more beautiful to stand beneath as you exchange your vows?"

I shook my head. I really couldn't. The arch I could see in my mind was perfect, and I knew Summer would make sure this one was every bit as beautiful as what I imagined.

Autumn grinned. "You like the place, don't you?"

I broke into a grin of my own and nodded my head. "I absolutely love it," I admitted.

"I knew you would," she said. "Come on, let's go meet Summer. You haven't even seen the best part yet."

Whatever the secret to this place was, I knew it must be good because both of the sisters actually agreed on it being the best part of the site.

I followed Autumn towards a side door I hadn't noticed before.

Autumn glanced over her shoulder at me. "I stick around because I'm a partner," she said.

"Huh?" I asked. Had I missed something?

"You asked me why I stay working for Summer. I don't work for her. She introduces me as her assistant and I go along with it because, quite honestly, life is too short to argue semantics. But I'm a partner in the business. She gets to make the final calls because she owns the larger share, but I'm not about to walk away from my own business and work for someone else."

Autumn's revelation surprised me. I was expecting her to say something about family loyalty, or that she owed Summer her help. But apparently it wasn't that after all. I couldn't quite see this mousey lady in front of me as a businesswoman. But then, people could surprise you.

Autumn led me outside of the church to where Summer was standing waiting for us.

"Do you like the arch?" Summer asked.

I nodded. "I absolutely loved it. I can see it in my mind," I gushed.

Summer laughed softly. "It's perfect, isn't it? But not quite as perfect as what's to come. Come on," she said excitedly.

I followed the two sisters down a short path and around a wall.

And then I saw it. I gasped, my jaw dropping open with shock. It was every bit as special as they had led me to believe. A large plunge pool sat beneath a flowing waterfall. Lilies floated on the surface of the pond and frogs hopped around it. The water was crystal clear and I could see small koi swimming lazily through it.

I could already imagine Billy and me standing right here in this spot, getting our photos taken, the waterfall in the background.

"I love it," I said. "I didn't expect to, but I do. I love all of it. Thank you, ladies."

2

I was sitting in the driver's seat of the truck, but I hadn't started the engine yet. I was content to relax for a moment and take in the atmosphere of the grounds of Hope Community. The more I thought about it, the more I realized that, actually, this was genuinely the perfect location for Billy and I to have our wedding. I was a little annoyed at myself for writing it off so completely in the beginning before even looking at it. It made me wonder what else I had missed out on. What other experiences would have been perfect but I had missed them because I had judged them with no real knowledge of what they were about and decided they weren't for me?

I pulled my cell phone out and texted Billy.

ME: Hope Community is perfect. U'll love it. I'll tell U everything when I see U. Are we still on 4 lunch?

BILLY: If U love it, I'll love it. And yes, we R. Can't wait to hear all the details.

I SMILED TO MYSELF. I loved that he trusted my judgement so completely.

I checked the time. I still had well over an hour before I would be meeting Billy for lunch so I decided to drop into Suzy's store and see her.

I put the truck into drive and headed away from the church, glancing back over my shoulder as I left. Who would have believed this place had such a magnificent view? And that waterfall was something else.

I thought about Suzy and baby Emma Rose. I was so happy when Suzy announced she was naming her baby after me. I mean, talk about the highest honor.

I had been surprised at first when Suzy had announced she was returning to working in the store so quickly after having Emma Rose, but the more I thought about it, the more it was Suzy all over. She was an excellent mom; she had taken to it like a natural. But she had always worked, and I knew sitting around waiting for Emma Rose to need feeding or changing would be driving her to despair. There was only so much cleaning a person could do around the house. So she took Emma Rose to the store with her each day, and there was rarely a moment when the baby wasn't being fussed over by one or another of Suzy's customers.

I parked the truck and hopped out. On a whim, I stopped at Bertie's Bakery and bought two cream donuts, before making my way down to Suzy's store, looking in the other shop windows as I went.

When I reached her store and slipped through the doorway, Suzy's face lit up at the sight of me and she darted out from behind the counter.

"I'm not coming to hug you. I saw the bag from Bertie's," she said with a laugh.

I laughed with her as she pulled me in for a hug.

"I'm kidding of course. How's the blushing bride? Did you fire that awful Summer Martin yet?"

"Of course not," I said. "It's not like she burned the church down."

"No, but she didn't take any notice of the kind of people you and Billy are, did she? Or she would never have tried to drag you up to Hope Community."

I had of course told Suzy about the venue issues and her advice had been to fire Summer.

"Actually, I think she knows our tastes exceptionally well," I said.

Suzy's eyebrows lifted in surprise. "You liked it?"

"Oh my gosh, Suzy. I loved it," I gushed.

I told her about the view, the waterfall and the way the inside of the church was laid out, including the amazing floral arch.

Suzy laughed and held her hands up. "Okay, I take it back. Don't fire her. She's good."

She looked pointedly at the bag in my hand. "So, now that's out of the way, how about we talk about the important things? Like donuts."

"How did you know they're donuts?" I laughed.

"Because I know you," she said as she held her hand out for the bag. "I'll go get us something to drink."

I was already heading for the nearby stroller before she was out of the room. I scooped Emma Rose up and hugged her close, breathing in deeply and smelling the gorgeous new baby smell of milk and baby powder.

"She smells a bit sweeter than she did at three o'clock this morning when she left me a poonami. Seriously, Emma, you have no idea how much mess there was. How does something so small create so much chaos?" Suzy called through from the break room.

I shook my head. "No idea," I said.

"It's just a good thing they're so cute," Suzy added.

I could hear her rattling around as she made us some coffee. She returned with two steaming mugs and two plates with the donuts on them.

"Do you want me to take her so you can eat your donut in peace?" Suzy asked.

I shook my head, holding Emma Rose a little tighter. "No way," I said. "I need my snuggly time."

Suzy laughed and bit into her donut.

"So, you've got your venue issues worked out. Is that the whole wedding planned and done then?" she asked when her mouth was no longer full.

"Pretty much," I said. "Billy and I are having lunch today, where we'll go over the favors and choose our favorite. We need to finalize the floral arrangements. And then it's just last minute stuff like make-up, hair and nails."

"Are you having a spray tan?" Suzy asked.

"I don't know yet." I shrugged. "Summer thinks I

should. She's booked me in for one, but I haven't decided whether or not I should go to the appointment."

"What's the worst thing that could happen?" Suzy asked.

"Umm, I could end up looking ridiculous," I said.

Suzy laughed with me.

"If Summer is as good as you say she is, she's not going to send you to a tanning shop full of amateurs. They'll know what color will best suit you, and it won't be bright orange."

We finished our coffee and donuts as we talked.

"Enough about me," I finally said. "Tell me about you. How are you coping with the no sleep thing?"

Suzy shrugged. "In some ways, it's not as bad as I expected, but in other ways, it's worse. She's in a fairly good routine, so there's that. I was worried she'd be one of those babies who are up all night. Obviously, it's good that she's not, but sometimes the routine is part of the problem. Like, I lay in bed unable to sleep, just watching the clock and counting down to the next time she'll be awake. And because I'm breastfeeding, I have to be up every time she is."

"It must be hard," I said. "Especially now you're back at work."

"Work is what keeps me sane, to be honest," Suzy said. "And I always have someone else scheduled to open the store, so I don't have the pressure of knowing I have to be here early if I don't want to be."

"It sounds like you've gotten it all worked out," I said.

"I don't know about that." Suzy laughed. "There's so much to learn and so much I hadn't even considered. It's definitely not something you can learn out of a book, Emma. I thought I was prepared. I'd read all of the baby books, practised diaper techniques, bathing, everything. And none of it works how you think it will. I'm definitely winging it. But do you know the best part of it all? I always thought it was a cliché when people say you don't know what love is until you have a baby. But it's true. Honestly, I have never ever felt love like this. That caught me completely by surprise, but in the most amazing way."

I smiled. It was obvious how much she adored Emma Rose. I could see it in the way she looked when she held her. How her eyes rarely left the baby whenever someone else was holding her. How she could talk about her for hours on end.

"How's Brian finding it all?" I asked.

"He loves being a dad, but just between me and you, I think he's a bit underwhelmed."

I raised an eyebrow. "How so?" I asked.

"You know Brian. He's hands on, and he's great with her. He changes diapers, bathes her and everything. But I think he's secretly looking forward to her being a bit older, so he can interact with her and play with her more."

I nodded. "Yeah, I get that. He'll love it when he can run around with her and teach her games."

"Exactly. Anyway, listen to me droning on about my life. You're about to get married, Emma. We should be talking about that. Are you excited?"

I smiled. "Yes, I really am. I mean, I'm nervous. Not about marrying Billy – I'm sure he's the one. But I'm nervous about the actual ceremony, you know? Like what if I fall over walking down the aisle, or what if I mess up my vows? But yes, I'm mostly excited."

"Try not to worry about stuff like that. It'll all be fine, and the day will fly by. Just try to relax and enjoy it."

"I will," I agreed.

"And I'll be right there by your side, so I'll make you a deal. If you do fall over, I'll throw myself on the ground with you and we can both look ridiculous together. How's that?"

"Perfect." I laughed.

Then I checked the time, shocked at how quickly the day was flying past.

"Well, I'd better go and meet Billy or his lunch break will be over before I get there," I said.

"Wow," Suzy said. "Is it that time already? Madam here will be wanting lunch herself soon."

She stood up and held her arms out for Emma Rose.

I handed her over somewhat reluctantly. I was definitely getting quite broody being around the baby so much and seeing the beautiful bond between her and Suzy.

"I can't wait to be a mom myself," I said.

"Oh, you'll be great at it. I'm already thinking about my next one."

We said our goodbyes and I went back to the truck.

I headed out towards Billy's place. I'd said I would go to the surgery so we had longer together, but Billy insisted on us having lunch at his house. He said he liked to be able to leave the surgery and break the day up a little bit, which I understood.

I pulled up outside of Billy's house, noting that his car was already there. I hopped out of my truck and went and rang the doorbell. It felt strange using the doorbell of a house I would be moving into soon.

Billy pulled the door open. Smiling warmly when he saw me, he leaned in and kissed me.

As I kissed him back, I noted the large knife in his hand.

"Do you always open the door prepared to be attacked?" I asked with a laugh, pointing to the knife in his hand, as he stepped aside and I walked in.

"What?" He looked down and realized what he was holding. "Oh, I didn't think. I've just finished making us some sandwiches. Go on out to the deck and I'll get rid of this and bring them out."

I walked through the living room and out of the patio doors onto the decking. The backyard was beautiful, so peaceful and cut off from the rest of the world. I sat watching bees dance among the honeysuckle as I waited for Billy.

I heard the door sliding open and I grinned up at him as he came outside. He carried a large tray with our sandwiches and a jug of lemonade with two glasses balanced rather precariously on it. I half stood to help him, but he shook his head and put the tray down on the table.

"See, I have the balancing skills," he said laughing.

He poured us both a glass of lemonade and I picked up my sandwich. It was perfect, a super soft bun packed with freshly roasted chicken, crispy lettuce and ripe, juicy tomatoes.

"This is lovely," I moaned as I bit into the sandwich.

"It's hardly culinary genius," he said.

"Compared to my skills in the kitchen, trust me it is." I laughed.

"So, tell me about this church," Billy said.

"Oh Billy, it's wonderful," I said. "The view from the front of it is divine. The gardens are beautiful, and through the trees, you can just glimpse the town. And behind it all, the mountains, purple and perfect. It's like a movie scene. Inside, it's all white and gold and the pews are this beautiful mahogany. The flowers will look amazing on them. There's even an arch for us to stand beneath to exchange our vows, and it'll be decorated with flowers."

He smiled at my enthusiasm. "You sound like you like it more than our original location," he said.

"You know what? I think I kind of do. You haven't even heard the best part yet. Around the back of the church, there's this secret garden. It's got a plunge pool covered with lilies and full of frogs and fish. And there's the most beautiful waterfall cascading down into it."

"It sounds perfect," he said. "I don't mean this to sound awful, I mean I'm not glad the original church burned down or anything, but I am glad we've changed the venue."

"You are?" I asked, a little surprised.

He nodded. "Yes. I know you liked the original church, but you weren't excited about it like you are about Hope Community. You weren't raving about how nice it was, how perfect everything would look."

"No, I guess I wasn't," I agreed. "I did like it, and I thought it was perfect at the time, but that's only because

I hadn't considered Hope Community Church as an option. I think this has shown me I need to be more open minded and give things I assume I won't like a chance."

"Maybe that's something we both should try more often," Billy mused.

"I called in to see Suzy earlier," I said, remembering the later part of my morning. "She's really taken to motherhood like a natural."

"There's nothing that woman can't do if she puts her mind to it," Billy said.

"That's true," I agreed.

"How's Emma Rose?"

"Gorgeous as always," I said. "She's so cute. Her little nose, her pink cheeks. She makes me want to just squeeze her and never let go."

"I think Suzy might be upset if you did." He laughed.

We finished the sandwiches and I drank some lemonade.

"Oh, I almost forgot. The wedding favors are in the truck. I told Summer we'd let her know today which ones we want. Would you mind grabbing the box from the back of the truck?"

"Not at all," Billy said.

He stood up, gathered our plates and headed inside. I got to my feet and stretched, feeling lazy after having spent half of the morning sitting around with Suzy and now sitting around out here too. I glanced through the dining room window, smiling to myself when I saw the stack of wedding presents there, waiting for us to open them later.

It would be like a fresh start for us, new things for a

new life. A life I would be sharing with Billy. I couldn't wait to get moved in after our honeymoon and start our lives together. This house was beautiful and it was already starting to feel like home.

Billy came back out to the patio with the box. He set it down on the ground and we sat cross-legged on the grass as he opened it up. We dug through the box, oohing and aahing at the various selections Summer had given us.

"Well?" I said.

"I'm not crazy about the ones with the chocolates," Billy answered. "The chocolates look nice enough, but they're not very personal, are they? I'd like to give our guests something to remember the day by, something they can keep."

"Me too," I agreed. "So the chocolates are out. I kind of like this one."

I held up the item that had caught my attention the second I spotted it: a small silver scroll. It had my name and Billy's name engraved in a heart and beneath it, the date of our wedding.

"Yes, me too," Billy said.

I grinned at him. I loved that we had the same tastes in things. The wedding planning had been a fun adventure we had shared, rather than a series of fights and compromises.

Billy's forehead furrowed in the way it always did when he was thinking.

"What is it?" I asked.

"I was just thinking. I do like the scroll and I think our guests will appreciate the sentiment, but I think it would be nice to also give them something for themselves. How about we ask Summer to combine the scrolls with something edible as well? Just to sort of give them a treat?"

"I think that's a lovely idea," I agreed. "Let's go whole hog and give them all a chocolate and salted caramel heart each, too."

Billy nodded and grinned.

"Yes, why not? We're only going to do this once, so let's do it right."

I reached out and squeezed his hand.

"I'll go call Summer now," I said.

I stood up, moved into the living room and called Summer. She answered with a curt "Summer Martin" almost as soon as the call connected.

"Hi Summer. It's Emma Hooper," I said.

"Emma, how great to hear from you. Is everything okay?"

"Oh yes, everything's great," I told her. "I just wanted to talk to you about the favors."

"Perfect. I wasn't expecting to hear from you so soon. I know you said today, but I'm very impressed with how efficient you are. You know, with some brides, I'm still chasing them for answers the day before their rehearsal dinner."

I shuddered at the thought of leaving something so important to the last minute like that.

"So which favors have you chosen?" she asked.

"Actually, we're wondering if it would be possible to combine two of them?"

"Of course," Summer said. "I have some darling little white boxes here that I can use to combine items in. The best part? The guests' names get added to each box. In gold. It will totally match the vibe of the church."

"Oh, that's great," I said.

It hit me again that it was almost like Hope Community had always been meant to be, like the universe was somehow telling me that was where our wedding should be held all along.

"We love the scrolls. We'd like them to be included, and a chocolate and salted caramel heart," I told her.

I could hear her tapping out the details on her tablet as I talked.

"Okay, all taken care of," Summer said when she had finished entering the info. "Now, don't forget about the meeting with the florist tomorrow."

"I haven't," I said. "I can't wait."

"Great. See you tomorrow, Emma. Have a fab day."

She cut the call off before I could respond and I laughed to myself as I went back out to the deck.

"It's all arranged," I told Billy. "I love Summer. She's so efficient." Then I remembered one thing I didn't love so much about her. "She treats Autumn terribly, though."

"Her assistant?" Billy asked.

"Well, here's the weird part. I thought Autumn was her assistant. That's what Summer introduces her as. But the photographer was late this morning, like two or three minutes late, so Summer went out to have words with him, as you can imagine. So, I got to talking with Autumn. Turns out, she lets it go that Summer introduces her as her assistant just to avoid an argument, but she's actually part owner of the business."

Billy raised an eye brow. "Wow. Talk about a plot

twist. I definitely didn't see that one coming. It explains why she sticks around, though, when Summer is so rude to her all the time."

"Yeah," I agreed. "I always wondered about that myself. Mystery solved."

"Are there any mysteries left in this town that you haven't solved?" He laughed.

"There might be one or two around still," I replied, grinning.

I took a long drink of my lemonade, while Billy changed the subject. "I'm afraid I have to get back to work. You can let yourself out whenever you're ready."

"I'll come along now," I said.

"Emma, you're going to live here after the wedding. You can stay here when I'm not home, you know."

I shrugged. "I know, but I have to get back to the farm anyway. I have a few things to do for my grandpa and then I have some design work to get to."

"Is your grandpa going to hire another farm hand?" Billy asked as we gathered up the jug, tray and glasses. "I mean, after Daniel's death and everything?"

"He already has," I told him. "But the new hand lives off the site and only comes in for the working day. And you know grandpa. There's so much he doesn't trust a stranger to take care of. He barely trusts me to do half of it, he's just too polite to say so."

"That sounds like Ed," Billy agreed. "He doesn't seem to understand the concept of retirement."

"True," I agreed. "And Grandma is no better."

"How's she doing?" Billy asked. "With her sleep-walking."

My grandma suffered episodes that we'd always referred to as her funny turns, where she would wander out of the house at night and often end up on the farmhouse roof, singing to the moon. We had recently discovered that they were a form of sleep walking and nothing to worry about.

"Grandpa has put a bolt on the back door and a security chain on the front door. They seem to fool her so she's not going outside anymore. But let me tell you, it's a very rude awakening hearing her singing her heart out in the kitchen in the middle of the night."

"I can imagine." Billy laughed. Then, he turned serious. "But it must be a relief for you and Ed to know she can't get outside and hurt herself. And no more clambering around on the roof to get her down."

I nodded. "Oh yes. It's much better, and Grandpa looks much less tired these days. I think he used to try and stay awake to make sure Grandma didn't come to any harm."

We went back into the house and I grabbed my purse while Billy took the used lunch things through to the kitchen. We walked down the hall and out of the house.

Billy kissed my cheek and said, "Right, back to it. I'll call you later, okay?"

"Okay," I agreed. "Have fun at work."

He grinned. "I will. I have Mr. Roberts coming in later to get a boil lanced. I can hardly wait."

I laughed. "You sure are living the high life."

He headed for his car and I got into my truck. He flashed his lights and gave me a wave.

After he left, I sat in the truck for a few moments, just

looking at Billy's beautiful house. It would be my house soon and the thought of it gave me goose bumps of excitement. I couldn't believe how much I had gained by returning to Hillbilly Hollow last year. Although I occasionally missed my old city life, I wouldn't swap my life here for the world.

3
———

I closed my laptop with a flourish, pleased with myself. I had managed to get a lot of my latest design project done yesterday afternoon, and having woken up early this morning, I'd gotten my chores done and then come back to my room, where I finished the design off. I hadn't planned to have it complete until tomorrow, but it felt good to be ahead of schedule for once.

Snowball looked up at me from her spot at the end of my bed as my laptop slammed shut. She gave a little bleat and I smiled sadly.

"I'm going to miss you, girl," I said.

She shuffled closer to me, lifting her head up so I could scratch beneath her chin. I obliged and she bleated happily, her little white stub of a tail wagging. I sat for a few minutes fussing over Snowball, feeling guilty that I would soon be leaving her behind.

I finally got off the bed and headed downstairs from

my attic bedroom, the little goat following me down the steps.

I took her through to the kitchen where my grandma stood stirring a large pot on the stove. The smell hit me immediately and made my mouth water, even though I had only had breakfast an hour ago.

"That smells delicious, Grandma," I said. "What is it?"

"Lamb stew," she replied. "For dinner tonight."

"Oh, I can't wait," I said.

I would miss Grandma's cooking, too. Billy was a good cook, but there was just something about Grandma's comfort food that always made me want to come back for more.

"Where are you off to?" Grandma asked, noting my shoes.

"I have to meet Summer and the florist," I explained. "Just to confirm everything for the floral arrangements. I shouldn't be gone too long. Do you need anything while I'm out?"

Grandma shook her head. "No thank you, dear," she said. "I'm planning on going into town myself later on today anyway. I'm meeting Margene Huffler and the girls for a coffee afternoon."

"Is that what you're calling your gossip sessions these days?" I teased her.

"It's not gossip, it's exchanging information," grandma said.

"Ah, okay." I smiled. "Well, I'd best get going or I'll be in for it with Summer. Leave me a list of chores for when I get back, okay?"

"Okay," Grandma agreed.

I leaned in and kissed her cheek and then I hurried out to my truck. I drove into town, lucky enough to find a parking spot close to Flower Power, the florist we were using for the wedding. I got out of the truck and made my way to the store.

Summer was waiting out front for me and she smiled when she saw me approaching her. She was alone this time.

She air kissed me when I reached her side. "Emma, dear, how are you? Excited? Nervous?"

"Both," I admitted. "It's so close now."

"It is," Summer agreed. She gestured to the store's doorway. "Shall we?"

I nodded.

"Where's Autumn?" I asked as Summer pulled the door to the store open and gestured for me to go in.

I nodded my thanks to her as I stepped in. She followed me, shutting the door quietly behind her.

"Autumn is off sorting out the favors," she said. "Don't you dare tell her I said this, but she's actually quite good at making those things look stunning."

I smiled. I thought it was the first nice thing I had heard her say about Autumn. The nice side of Summer soon fell away, though, when we reached the counter of the store and found it unmanned. Summer banged her hand hard on the counter and I cringed.

"Doris? Doris? Get out here," she demanded loudly.

Doris Young, the florist who owned Flower Power, appeared out of a side door.

"Ah, Summer. Always a pleasure to see you," she said.

It was clearly a lie, a lie Doris made no attempt to make sound even vaguely true.

Summer rolled her eyes. "I wish I could say the same thing, but as always, you are inefficient."

"Excuse me?" Doris said, raising an eyebrow.

"You knew what time we'd be here. Why weren't you waiting for us?"

"Because some of us have real jobs and we can't just stand around looking pretty all day."

Doris turned away from Summer before she could respond and smiled at me, a genuine smile this time. "How are you, Emma?"

"Good, thank you. And you?"

"Great," Doris said. "I can't wait to show you the final plans for your arrangements. Come on through."

I'd only met Doris once before today, but she greeted me like an old friend. I liked her. She was friendly, and her arrangements were always stunning. It said a lot about her skills as a florist that Summer used her services, even though the two women clearly didn't like each other.

I followed Doris through to the back of the store with Summer behind me. The back room was cold, refrigerated to keep the flowers cool and fresh. Doris led me through the room, weaving between shelves and stands loaded down with beautiful flowers of every color of the rainbow. She headed towards a table adorned with a lovely yellow and pink bouquet.

She glanced back at me and I tried to smile, but she instantly saw something was wrong.

"What is it?" she asked.

"I ... they're beautiful," I said, nodding towards the bouquet. "But they're not the colors we talked about."

Summer instantly bristled, moving to step around me, but before she could intervene, Doris laughed softly.

"Good thing they're not for you then, isn't it?" she said.

I felt my cheeks blush, embarrassed at my mistake.

Doris saw my embarrassment and brushed off my apology before I could get it out.

"It's fine," she said. "I get it. We were heading towards them, and I know a lot of the less conscientious florists would have your arrangements made up by now. But I don't work that way, honey. When I say fresh flowers, I mean fresh flowers. I've put together a mock up to show you, but your real arrangements will be put together the night before your wedding and taken to your venue first thing."

I nodded. "Thank you," I said.

Doris turned to Summer then. "That reminds me, Summer. I need you to find out what time I can get into Hope Community on the day."

Summer instantly pulled out her tablet and touched the screen a few times.

"Any time after nine. Will that give you enough time, or do you need me to put pressure on them to let you in earlier?"

"Nine is fine," Doris said.

She led me past the yellow and pink bouquet and through another door.

"Here we are," she announced.

She was pointing to a beautiful arrangement of white

roses with a green and white spray. Two large red roses where set in the arrangement, complementing the white and really bringing the whole thing to life.

I gasped and my hands went to my mouth. "It's absolutely perfect," I said.

"Don't sound so surprised." Doris laughed.

"Right," Summer snapped, her tablet out again. "We'll need everything we talked about last time, plus an extra twelve pew toppers due to the change of location, and a floral archway."

She turned her tablet around and showed it to Doris.

"This is the arch. It needs to match the others. Plenty of red but not enough to be gaudy. Mostly white with some cherry blossoms and some greenery. And we need the bride's bouquet and one for her matron of honor. Is that clear? Do you think you can manage it?"

I could see Doris was offended at Summer's abrupt manner.

"Of course I can manage that," she snapped. "Do you think I'm totally incompetent?"

Summer opened her mouth to reply and I knew the answer wouldn't be complimentary and would only make the atmosphere in here even more awkward.

"Doris, do you have a bouquet of a similar size to mine?" I cut in quickly. "I'd just like to hold it and feel the weight so I can see how it will feel on the day."

Summer's cell phone rang. She snatched it from her pocket and checked the screen.

"It's the caterer. I have to take this. Would you excuse me, Emma?"

"Of course," I said.

Summer hurried away, already taking the call. I waited until she was out of earshot.

"I'm sorry about that," I said.

Doris laughed. "Don't worry, it's not your fault. I pay her no mind. She's always like that. Between you and me, I think she's watched too many of those wedding movies where the wedding planner is always a brat."

I couldn't help but laugh although I did feel kind of guilty for laughing at Summer. She was mean, there was no question about that, but she got things done, and she'd never been anything but pleasant to me and Billy.

"Right, let's find you a bouquet," Doris said.

"Actually, it's fine. I'm pretty sure I can hold a bunch of flowers without practising it. I just wanted to stop you and Summer from killing each other."

"Oh, I see," Doris laughed. "One day it might just come to that. That's the only problem with small towns. You can't be picky about who you do business with."

Summer came marching back, her heels clacking.

"Did you manage okay, Emma?" she asked.

I nodded. "Yes. Is everything alright with the caterer?"

"Of course," Summer said. "Everything's fine with everyone. That's what I'm here for. Now don't you go worrying about that or anything else, okay? The only thing I want you focusing on now is getting a good night's sleep each night between now and the wedding."

That could be easier said than done with my work and Grandma's singing, but I nodded anyway.

"Are we all clear here then or is there anything else you need to show us or ask Emma about?" Summer asked Doris.

"No, all good," Doris replied. She turned to me. "Emma? Do you have any questions or is there anything you want to see?"

I shook my head. "I don't think so."

"Well, if you think of anything you can give me a call. Or Summer can advise you, I'm sure."

As we left the store, Summer said, "Now, I meant what I said in there. I don't want you to worry about anything, Emma. Everything will be perfect on the day, but if you do think of anything that concerns you, I'm available twenty-four seven. Don't be afraid to call me."

"Thank you," I said.

It was still a shock to my system the way Summer switched between her two personalities, the nasty one she seemed to save for everyone she worked with, and the nice one she reserved for clients only.

She hugged me and sauntered off towards her car, her hips swishing in her tight pencil skirt.

I texted Billy as I walked back to my truck.

ME: The flowers R beautiful and Summer has arranged for us 2 have extra pew toppers because the church is so much bigger.

BILLY: Perfect. I can't wait 2 marry U.

ME: I can't wait either. Everything is set. Just fingers crossed nothing goes wrong.

BILLY: It won't.

. . .

I HOPED HE WAS RIGHT. He would be I was sure. As if Summer would allow anything to go wrong.

I felt good as I got back into my truck and headed for the farm.

After arriving at home, I parked my truck and headed inside. I entered through the front door into a house that had that empty feeling you always get when no one is home.

"Grandma? Grandpa?" I called as I walked through the living room towards the kitchen, checking to make sure I had been right. I didn't want to march into the kitchen and scare one of my grandparents half to death if they hadn't heard me coming in.

The only answer I got to my shout was an excited bleat as Snowball came trotting out of the kitchen to greet me. I hadn't really expected an answer from either of my grandparents. Grandma would still be in town, and Grandpa would be out in the fields somewhere tending to the farm, but it was always best to double-check these things.

I dropped to a crouch and scratched behind Snowball's ears and underneath her chin. Her little white fluff ball of a tail wagged excitedly and I laughed, struck once more by how much like a dog she was. She was loyal, always sticking by my side, and she loved attention and treats. Everything I associated with a dog.

"Looks like it's just me and you, girl," I said to her, straightening up and wincing when my back cracked loudly.

Snowball gave an alarmed bleat and I couldn't help but laugh at her reaction. It had definitely been a loud crack and I couldn't blame her for being a little alarmed by it.

"Let's go and see what jobs Grandma has left me," I added.

I went to the fridge, Snowball hot on my heels. It was all I could do to avoid tripping over her. I was really going to miss her when I moved into Billy's place. I hoped she wouldn't miss me too much. She would still have Grandma, of course, who fed her treats constantly. All the same, it was a shame that Grandma had never managed to tame Molly, the barn owl who lived in our barn. It would have been nice for Snowball to have a friend around the place when my grandparents were busy.

Pinned to the fridge I found a scrawled note in Grandma's handwriting. Taking it down, I smiled and shook my head. Instead of a list of chores, she'd left me a message: "You're getting married soon. Just relax and look forward to your wedding."

It was sweet of her, and the gesture made me smile, but while I was still here, I intended to make myself useful. I wandered out to the back of the farm with Snowball still trotting along beside me. I looked around. The chickens had already been fed and their eggs collected, and I knew Grandpa had his own strict routine when it came to the larger animals. I decided to settle for weeding the vegetable patch and the flower beds and sweeping the yard. They weren't majorly pressing tasks but things that needed doing. Anyway, it would save my grandma some work.

I made my way over to the barn with Snowball beside me and went in.

"Hey Molly," I said as the owl screeched out what I liked to think of as a greeting but what was much more likely to be a complaint at being disturbed.

I gathered up a pair of tough gardening gloves, a hoe, a hand fork, the sweeping brush and a shovel and a thick black garbage sack. Then I made my way back to the backyard area.

When I got down on my knees and slipped the gloves on, Snowball instantly put her front hooves on my lap, thinking I was going to give her some more scratching. I tried to stroke her, but she looked at me with an almost human expression that said *I don't think so* when the gloves touched her.

She moved back out of my reach and stood watch over me as I began to weed the first vegetable patch. She kept looking at the gloves and then looking at me, almost as though she was trying to convince herself they were definitely not a permanent fixture. I didn't much like the feel of them either, and they were far from permanent as far as I was concerned. I actually preferred the feeling of the earth beneath my hands, but I wasn't going to risk blistering my palms or breaking my nails so close to my wedding. I wanted my hands to look soft and beautiful on the big day.

I soon began to wish I'd brought one of Grandma's old cushions to kneel on as the hard ground hurt my knees, but I was reluctant to go all the way back to the barn to get one. I would just have to suck it up. I told myself the faster I got done, the faster I could be back on my feet and off my knees. The thought spurred me on a little bit and I made quick and efficient progress around the area.

As I weeded and turned the ground over, I thought back to the time I had spent here on the farm. Firstly, there was me growing up here with my grandparents after my parents were killed in a car wreck, and then returning here after my own accident. It had always been my happy place, this house. It had always been filled with the hustle and bustle of an honest day's work and the laughter of a happy life.

I knew I would be sad to leave it all behind. It wasn't just Snowball I would miss. It was my grandparents and their home, my home, as well. It was like the end of an era. I also knew it was the only way. It was time to look to my future and I felt a rush of happiness as I thought of Billy and a flash of excitement at the thought of finally living with him.

Yes, I would miss this place, my grandparents, Snowball, Molly. Even the chickens. But I would only be a couple of minutes down the road in town, and I would visit often. Probably too often. Billy would be at work all day, and because I could set my own hours, there would be nothing to stop me visiting daily if my grandparents needed my help. Or if I wanted to use that as an excuse to come over regularly.

Even though Billy's house was soon to become my home, a part of me knew that this place would always be home deep down in my heart as well.

4

I was practically skipping as I made my way along Main Street. I had been for a quick coffee with Suzy and of course a big hug off little Emma Rose who had made the cutest little gurgling sounds as I held her. She had blinked up at me with her beautiful blue eyes, her long black eyelashes eventually lying on her cheeks as she had fallen asleep in my arms. I was almost jealous of those eyelashes. I needed mascara just to show people I actually had eyelashes and not just stumps.

Suzy had spent most of the visit listening to me as I babbled on about this and that and everything. I was turning into a nervous wreck. My wedding was in two days' time and I was an almost constant mix of excitement and nervous energy.

I had even been singing to myself this morning as I mucked out the pig sty and cleaned the chicken coop, definitely not my favorite jobs in the world. Somehow knowing I was about to become Mrs. Emma Stone made even the most mundane tasks seem like something I could enjoy. I was happy, that was the main thing of it all. Billy made me happy. And now I knew I would be his forever.

I had plenty of chores around the farm and design tasks for my business, enough to keep me busy and my mind occupied. But for the first time, I was starting to regret having a wedding planner. It was good in some ways to know that if there was a problem Summer would be there to fix it for me. But in other ways, it left me at a bit of a loose end, and I was a little worried that something would go wrong without me knowing about it.

I had been checking in regularly with Summer, who was quick to reassure me. Even though I was sure my calls were a nuisance to her, she had never once made me feel like I was bothering her or tried to stop me from calling.

I had called her again this morning, as had been my standard thing for the last few days, but she hadn't answered this time. It was very unlike her, and it gave me an uneasy feeling, like maybe something had gone wrong, something so big that she was still trying to work out how to break it to me.

The rational part of my mind knew I was being crazy. I knew that she was a busy woman and she was most likely stuck in meetings or something rather than purposefully avoiding my calls. But still, it gave me something to focus my energy on, the worrying.

I had decided if she hadn't called me back by one o'clock, then I would call Autumn. I was sure Autumn wouldn't screen my calls, and even if I couldn't get her to spill everything, I would know by her voice and the way she handled my questions whether I really had something to worry about or not.

I had just reached my truck when my cell phone buzzed in my pocket and I felt a flood of relief. Summer must have been in a meeting or with a client or something, that was all, and now she was calling me back.

I glanced at the screen and frowned when I saw Billy's name there instead of Summer's. I checked the time. It was eleven fifteen and Billy should have been mid surgery, not calling me. Something was most definitely wrong, and this time I knew I wasn't being paranoid.

"What's happened?" I demanded as I answered the call.

"How did you know something happened?" Billy asked.

His words did nothing to quell the panic rising inside of me. He hadn't reassured me everything was okay; he'd just asked how I had known there was a problem. It meant I was right. Something was very wrong. Hearing his normal voice did ease my worries about him, though. It didn't sound like he was hurt or sick or anything. He wouldn't sound quite so normal if something was the matter with him.

"You wouldn't be calling me in the middle of your surgery if nothing had happened," I replied, answering his question.

I wanted to ignore it and demand he just tell me what was going on, but at the same time, I wanted to buy myself a little more time. A little more time where I was ignorant of whatever had gone wrong so I could stay happy for a moment longer.

Billy said. "Okay, Emma. Are you sitting down?"

This was getting worse by the moment. Something really bad had to have happened for him to need me to be sitting down. My thoughts went immediately to my grandparents. If either of them were hurt Billy, as the town doctor, would no doubt have been called to attend. And he would want to be the one to tell me, rather than leaving it to Sheriff Tucker or a stranger from the hospital.

"My grandparents...?"

I trailed off, not wanting to finish the sentence, afraid of the answer I might hear.

"They're fine," Billy finished. "Are you sitting down?"

There was that question again. The sentence people always used to prepare you for something really bad.

"No," I snapped, getting impatient now. "I'm just about to get into my truck. Just tell me what it is."

He had assured me my grandparents were fine. He was obviously okay and I knew Suzy and Emma Rose were both good because I had just left them. What else could be wrong that I couldn't cope with? I could deal with this standing up.

Then, a thought struck me. What if it was Brian? What if I had to go and tell Suzy something bad had happened to Brian?

"Emma, Summer Martin has been killed," Billy said quietly.

His words silenced my fears about Brian, but they brought with them a whole new set of emotions and problems. My head spun and I reached out a hand, resting it on the side of the truck to steady myself until the dizziness passed.

"Summer Martin as in our wedding planner?" I asked, sure I had somehow misunderstood.

"Yes," Billy confirmed.

"How?" I asked. "What happened?"

My mind was racing. Was this somehow my fault? I had momentarily wished I didn't have a wedding planner, and now I didn't.

You're being ridiculous, Emma, I told myself. *Your fleeting thoughts couldn't kill a woman.*

I still felt guilty, though, not least because my first concern upon hearing the news was for our wedding. I had no idea who Summer had booked for half of the things. I didn't know where my dress would be coming from or where it would be sent to. I didn't know who was doing the catering, or how to contact the band. I didn't know anything. Not even who to contact at the church on the day to collect the keys and let Doris the florist in.

They weren't the thoughts you were supposed to have upon hearing of a death. You were meant to feel sad for the person who had died, sad for the friends and family they had left behind. I was sure that would come later.

"Emma?" Billy said. "Are you alright?"

I took a deep breath and let it slowly.

"Yes, I'm fine," I said. "This is just so unexpected."

It would all be okay. I could make this work. Autumn would surely have a copy of our wedding folder, or at least know where it was. I could work everything out myself from that.

My mind was already whirling, so full of details that it

took me a moment to realize Billy hadn't answered my question from a moment ago.

"What happened to Summer?" I repeated.

"Tucker got a call saying there had been an accident. He rushed to the scene to find Summer's car crashed into a wall. She must have been driving pretty fast. The front end was smashed to pieces. She was in a bad way, but she was alive. Tucker called an ambulance and then me because he knew I was here in town and might get there faster. I did get there first but was too late to save her. She was dead by the time I arrived. And there's more. It looks like it wasn't really an accident, at least according to what I overheard Tucker saying."

"What do you mean?" I asked.

"Her brakes had been cut," Billy replied.

My mind was spinning again. Everyone in town knew Summer's distinctive white sports car. And everyone knew she liked to drive it too fast. It probably wouldn't take much work cutting her brake cables.

"Tucker said the way they were damaged showed they had broken down gradually," Billy went on. "Whoever was responsible did it in a way that meant the brakes wouldn't fail immediately, that she'd have to get up enough speed to shake them lose, meaning they would fail right at the moment she needed them most."

"Wow," I breathed. "She could have hit another car, or ploughed through a bus line of people. Whoever did this to her wanted her dead badly enough that they didn't care who she took out with her. Does Tucker have any idea who it was?"

"No," Billy said. "But that's not your problem, Emma.

Just let Tucker deal with this one. You have more than enough on your plate with work and the farm. And now the last minute jobs for the wedding."

"I know. I won't get involved," I promised him. "I was just curious. Billy, so many people hated her it would be hard to narrow it down to even a reasonably short list, let alone a single suspect."

"I know, but there's a difference between hating to deal with someone and having a plausible reason to kill them."

"True," I agreed.

"Listen, Emma, I have to go. Will you be alright?"

"Yes, of course," I said. "I'm going to head home and get some work done, and then tomorrow I'll call Autumn and ask for our folder. I know it's insensitive when her sister has just died, but I think she'll understand."

"Okay, honey. Talk to you later," Billy said before ending the call. I realized he was probably shaken himself and needed time to settle down after the scene he had just come from.

I drove back to the farm in a state of disbelief. How could Summer be dead? Who would have done such a thing? My mind went to Derrick Williams, our wedding photographer. Autumn had made a joke about him snapping one day and killing Summer. It didn't seem quite so funny now, but it also didn't mean he had actually killed her. Everyone made throw away statements like that at times. Ninety-nine times out of a hundred, they meant absolutely nothing.

I parked the truck and went inside the farm house, trying to silence the side of my brain that was begging me to start investigating Summer's murder. I had told Billy I wouldn't get involved and I had meant it. I had far too much to do already. I would leave this one to Tucker.

I wasn't overly confident the sheriff would be able to find out any sort of satisfactory answer, but I wasn't confident I would either. Not with Summer. Not when she had treated so many people badly at one time or another. Maybe I could …

No, stop it. Don't get involved Emma.

I gritted my teeth and pushed my questions aside, as I walked into the house and through to the kitchen, where I could hear my grandma making lunch. Snowball bleated and came running towards me as I walked in.

My grandma turned around, smiling a greeting at me. The smile froze on her face as she looked at me.

"Emma, you're as white as a sheet. Whatever is the matter?" she asked.

"I'm fine, Grandma," I said.

She ignored my protests and led me to a chair. I sat down heavily.

"I'm going to make some sweet tea. You just wait there a minute and then you can tell me what has got you in such a state."

She turned to the kettle and switched it on and then she started collecting up tea bags, sugar, and a pitcher full of ice. I sat silently watching her as she made our tea, absently stroking Snowball who had plonked her little head in my lap the moment I sat down.

"It's not Suzy or the baby is it?" my grandma asked.

I shook my head. "No, they're both fine," I said.

My grandma finished preparing the tea and sat down beside me, pushing a cold glass towards me.

"Drink," she ordered.

I took a mouthful of the icy brew and had to admit that it made me feel a little better. More relaxed. I swallowed another mouthful.

"Summer Martin is dead," I finally said between sips.

"Who's Summer ...? Oh. You're wedding planner," Grandma said, answering her own question as the realization dawned on her.

"Yes," I confirmed.

"What happened?" Grandma asked.

"Tucker told Billy that someone cut her brakes. Her car crashed. She died before Billy could get there," I explained.

"Oh, Emma. I'm so sorry," Grandma said, reaching out and squeezing my hand. "The news must have come as quite a shock to you."

"It did," I admitted. "But I'm fine. Really. I mean it's not like we were friends or anything."

"I hate to sound callous, but what will happen about the wedding?" Grandma asked.

"Autumn, Summer's sister, who I thought was her assistant is actually her business partner. Now obviously she's just lost her sister and she's not going to feel like taking over so soon after her death, but I'm hoping she at least has access to my folder with all of the information in it. I'm going to have to call her tomorrow and ask for it, as insensitive as that is. And then I can work out what needs doing and get on with it," I said.

"I'm sure she won't think it's insensitive. If she is a

partner in the business, she must know this means she's going to have to step up. Most people would have been on the phone to her by now demanding to know what's going to happen. She'll probably just be relieved that you're being so reasonable about it all," Grandma said.

"I hope so," I agreed.

As we finished the rest of our tea, I explained to Grandma that as far as I was aware, everything was in place for the wedding. I mostly just needed contact numbers for everyone to confirm times and last minute things. I would need to call all of the contacts, though, just to advise them of my cell phone number and to tell them they would need to call me rather than Summer if they needed anything or if there were any problems. I prayed there wouldn't be. Surely this was a big enough problem in and of itself without anything else happening. I had to cling to that hope, although I wasn't confident it would work out that way with Summer out of the picture.

I got up from the table and picked up our used glasses. Grandma tried to take them from me but I smiled and shook my head.

"Really, Grandma, I'm fine," I insisted. "I'm going to rinse these glasses and run out to the outhouse, and then, unless you need me for anything, I'm going to push on with work and try to clear it up so I'm free to concentrate on wedding stuff."

"No I don't need you, honey. Everything is under control here." Grandma smiled.

I rinsed the glasses out at the sink and dried them,

Snowball sticking to my heels as I moved around the kitchen. Grandma smiled at her antics.

"She knows you'll be leaving us soon. She wants to make the most of you while she can," she commented.

"I'm sure she'll be just fine without me, getting spoiled by you." I laughed. "And I'll only be down the road. You'll never be fully rid of me."

I headed for the back door.

"Good." Grandma beamed. She cleared her throat. "If you spot your grandpa while you're outside tell him his lunch is ready, will you?"

"Will do," I said.

"Do you want anything, Emma? I can make you a sandwich or something if you'd like."

I shook my head. "No thank you. I already ate with Suzy," I lied.

If I told her the truth, that I wasn't really hungry, she would only worry about me, and I would never be able to convince her it wasn't because of Summer.

I stepped out into the yard and Snowball ran ahead of me. I spotted my grandpa straight away over by the barn and hurried over to give him Grandma's message.

"Great," he said. "I'm starving."

He started for the house and turned back to me when he realized I wasn't following.

"Are you not coming in? Your grandma won't be happy if you keep her waiting," he said.

I laughed. "Oh believe me, I'm not brave enough to keep her waiting. I've already grabbed a bite with Suzy."

He nodded and walked to the house.

I went back towards the outhouse. My cell phone

vibrated in my pocket and I pulled it out, wondering if Billy had some news on the culprit of Summer's murder. But it wasn't Billy calling. It was Autumn Martin, Summer's sister. I was shocked to see her name, and I wondered for one horrible minute if no one had told her yet.

I dismissed the thought. Tucker was far from being an excellent Sheriff – someone could be murdered while he was in the room and he would still get the conclusion wrong as to who had done it – but he wasn't lax when it came to notifying people of a situation. He would have talked to Autumn already.

I took the call.

"Hello," I said.

"Emma? I take it you've heard about Summer, since Billy was with the sheriff when he came to give me the news."

"I have. I'm so sorry, Autumn," I said.

She didn't respond and the silence stretched out. I waited and when it was clear she wasn't going to answer me, I pushed on.

"I was actually going to call you tomorrow. I wondered if I would be able to collect my folder," I said.

"Really?" Autumn asked, sounding surprised. "My sister just died and you're firing me?"

"What? No of course I'm not firing you. You and Summer have done all of the work, and of course you'll still be getting paid. I just thought with what had happened, that I would need to take care of any last minute details," I said.

Autumn sniffed loudly. "I'm sorry, I shouldn't have

snapped at you like that," she said. "Thank you for
thinking of me that way, but unless you have any objec-
tions, I was actually calling you to confirm that I would
be taking over the last minute arrangements and coordi-
nating the day."

"I didn't think you'd feel like doing it," I said. "Honestly Autumn, please don't feel like you have to do this.
I'd understand, and ..."

"My sister and I had our issues, as you know,"
Autumn interrupted me. "But we were always together,
and I need something to focus on. Something to stop me
from just sitting around moping. And this is what
Summer would have wanted."

I nodded my head, although I was aware that Autumn
couldn't see me. What she was saying made perfect sense,
and I thought that in her position I might feel exactly the
same way.

"If you're sure, that would be great," I said. "But look,
if it gets too much, you only have to let me know. Okay?"

"I will. Thank you, Emma," she said. "I'm going
through your folder now. I've worked closely with
Summer on this one so I'm up to speed with what needs
doing. I'm just double checking everything. But you can
relax. You're in good hands, Emma."

"Thank you," I said.

"Call me anytime, hon. And if I don't hear from you,
I'll see you bright and early on the morning of your
wedding."

She ended the call. I frowned at my cell phone for a
moment before I put it away, like it would somehow have
the answers. I was still kind of shocked at the call with

Autumn, although I was relieved to know I wouldn't have to spend my time chasing wedding details. As much as I had thought I was ready for it, when it had nearly became a reality, I could instantly feel the weight of it all pressing down on me, stressing me out.

I pulled my phone back out and sent Billy a text, explaining to him that Autumn was taking over the wedding planning. I guessed my grandma was right. Autumn was a partner in the business, now most likely the full owner, and she understood one thing: no matter what happens, if you want your business to be a success, then the show must go on.

5

I came back out of the outhouse to a rather indignant Snowball who looked at me and bleated.

I laughed and shook my head. "I draw the line at you going in there with me," I told her.

She seemed to be appeased by my simple statement and she trotted over to examine a particularly tasty looking dandelion. She sneezed as she sniffed at it, and I laughed to myself. It didn't put her off, and she promptly gobbled down the dandelion in one big bite. I started walking back towards the house and Snowball trotted over to me, running in circles around me as I walked.

Suddenly, the little goat stopped and sniffed the air. She moved away from me, putting a couple of feet of distance between us. I looked where she was heading. I didn't see anything that could have caught her attention, but she was a curious little creature and she often took a keen interest in a particular blade of grass that looked no different to me than any of the other blades of grass. I thought nothing of her strange behaviour until she lay down flat on her belly and stared at a patch of air before me.

That was when I knew. I was about to get a visit from a ghost, and I would bet my last cent that it would be the ghost of Summer Martin.

I had barely formed the thought when the air in front of me began to shimmer. I'd never seen a ghost exactly shimmer before. I frowned, sure I was mistaken, but I wasn't. As I watched, my mouth hanging open in surprise, Summer materialised in front of me.

She didn't speak, didn't do anything. She just kind of hovered there. I wasn't quite sure what to do, so I did the only thing I could think of and sidestepped around her. She turned as I passed her and floated along at my side.

"Please stop following me," I said.

The ghost of Summer laughed, a cold, almost cruel laugh.

"I will. Once you get to the bottom of my murder and find out who's responsible," she replied. "I want justice and I won't rest until I get it."

By now, I was used to ghosts showing up, asking me to resolve the mysterious circumstances of their deaths. It was a gift I had, the ability to see and speak to the dead. I had fallen into the role of "ghost detective" some time ago, and was hardly ever unsettled anymore by the arrival of a ghostly being with a request like Summer's.

Still, with my wedding approaching, the timing couldn't be worse.

"I understand how you feel," I said. "But in case you've forgotten, I have a wedding in two days."

"I haven't forgotten. Just like I haven't forgotten where

your honeymoon is. And if you don't solve this murder, I'll be coming with you."

She faded back away as quickly as she had come before I had time to reply. I was sure she was no longer following me once Snowball got to her feet again and ran back to me. She never wanted to be close to me when I had one of my ghostly visitors, but the second they left she was back at my side.

"Oh, Snowball, what am I going to do about this?" I asked her.

I got a loud bleat in response.

"Yes, you're right," I said. "It's that simple. I just have to find the murderer in the next two days, along with getting through my design work and my chores on the farm. Oh yes, and fit in enough sleep that I don't end up with big bags under my eyes on my wedding day."

Now that Autumn had decided to take over the wedding stuff I would have a little spare time. The time I had feared I would have to use calling contractors and vendors could be used instead to start doing a little digging.

As I passed through the kitchen and said a quick hello and goodbye to my grandparents, it occurred to me that I had known from the second Billy had said Summer had been murdered that this would be what came next. I had known even when I told Billy I'd be staying out of the investigation that I would be looking into it.

I went up to the attic with Snowball at my heels and sat down on my bed. After opening my laptop, I thought for a moment, then opened a blank document and quickly typed up what I knew about Summer's murder. It didn't help much. Her car was conspicuous and well known and it was common knowledge that, to Summer, speed limits were a mere suggestion.

My mind kept going back to Derrick Williams, the photographer, and Autumn's words about him. She was obviously joking, but was it too much of a stretch to think he'd finally gotten sick of being berated by Summer and snapped? After all, someone had to have killed her, didn't they?

Out of morbid curiosity, I opened my web browser and typed Derrick's name and "Hillbilly Hollow" into the search box. I was expecting a social media profile or a website for his business. I got both of those, but what caught my attention were the newspaper stories. I frowned and clicked on one.

As I skimmed through the article, I felt my jaw dropping. Derrick Williams had a record. Twelve years ago, he had been given a two month suspended jail sentence for stalking an ex-girlfriend. There wasn't much information other than that in the article and I quickly clicked out of it and into another.

This one wasn't truly an article but a post on the town's small online message board, so had information of a gossipier nature. It seemed like Derrick's girlfriend had dumped him and Derrick had then followed the woman whenever she went out. Eventually, she had tired of asking him to leave her alone and sought a restraining order, which was promptly granted. But Derrick had broken it by approaching her again, hence the suspended sentence.

Wow, I thought to myself. This man was going to be

the photographer at our wedding and he sounded like a nut. Apparently, his lawyer had played the case that he had no intention of harming the woman, he was merely so deeply in love with her that he couldn't let her go. Had a part of him felt that way about Summer Martin? Had he given up on getting her back and killed her so she couldn't move on without him?

No, I thought, Autumn had specifically told me that he had ended the relationship with Summer. He was clearly unhinged, though, and surely that made him more likely to snap and resort to such an extreme reaction. I wasn't sure. There was no record of him being violent to the woman, and murder was a far cry from watching someone. He was still a long way from leaving my top suspect list, all the same.

Out of interest, I clicked through to his social media profile. He had updated his status that morning: *Meeting with the Martin dragon today. Wish me luck.*

My jaw dropped again. He had known for sure that Summer would be out and about in her car today as she was meeting him. While part of me screamed that it had to be him, another, more reasonable part of me said to slow down and think. If he had planned on Summer having an accident today, would he really have broadcast his meeting with her so publicly? And made it so clear he didn't have the best relationship with her?

Surely not. Whoever cut those brake cables must have known that it would be noticed and that the sheriff would be looking into it as a murder. But maybe if they knew Tucker, they wouldn't have been overly worried about that. And they wouldn't have banked on me getting involved.

I forced myself to calm down. I added the facts and only the facts next to Derrick Williams' name in my document, under the heading "suspects".

I sat for a moment, looking at his name. Did I really want this man to be a part of my wedding? What if he had killed Summer?

I told myself once more to calm down. There was no proof he had killed Summer.

I couldn't afford to fire him now. Where would I find another photographer at such short notice? And how would I explain it to Autumn without accusing him of murder with no proof? Plus, said the detective voice in my head, it would be a good opportunity to watch him. Keep him close and keep an eye on him.

I couldn't help but snort out a bitter laugh as another thought occurred to me.

Snowball looked up at me as I laughed and I shook my head.

"Don't worry, Snowball. I haven't quite lost my mind yet, I promise," I said.

The thought that had occurred to me was a simple yet true point. If I fired Derrick from my wedding based solely on the fact that he wasn't exactly a fan of Summer, I would have to fire every single person, from the florist to the caterer to my wedding dress maker.

My laughter subsided as Doris Young, the florist, popped into my head again. She had made no secret of the fact she didn't like Summer. Maybe she had finally had enough of being spoken to like she was a naughty child in her own business. Maybe she had decided to get Summer out of the way, leaving her free and clear to deal with the mousey Autumn.

I did a web search for Doris's name, but I found nothing except a website for Flower Power. I sat thinking. I remembered my last investigation when I wanted to know if there was any dirt on a potential suspect. I hadn't wanted to involve my grandma, the town's biggest gossip, so I had called the next best person; Margene Huffler. Margene was a friend of my grandma's, as well as being the mother of Prudence Marianne Huffler, who I'd once been involved in a case with.

If Doris had anything real against Summer, or indeed if anyone did, Margene would know. I just needed a reasonable cover story. It didn't have to be overly detailed. Margene needed no excuse to talk.

I thought for a moment and then I reached into my pocket for my cell phone and called her. She answered quickly.

"Hi Emma. How's the wedding planning going?" she asked.

"Actually, that's what I wanted to talk to you about," I said.

"Really?" Margene asked, sounding pleased that I was asking for her opinion on any part of my wedding. I suspected she sometimes got lonely, since her daughter had recently moved out of state and settled in far away Faerywood Falls, Colorado.

"My wedding planner has been murdered," I said.

I paused for a moment letting this sink in. Margene gasped. I could almost hear the glee in her gasp as she pictured herself telling everyone that she knew before they did.

"I'm a little worried that something could happen at my wedding. I wondered if you'd be able to help me. I need to know if someone had a specific grudge against her, or if it's someone targeting my wedding."

"Oh, Emma, I'm sure it's not anyone trying to make trouble for your wedding. But if you can give me your wedding planner's name, I can try and think if I know of anyone who might dislike her enough to hurt her. It's an extreme measure though, isn't it? Maybe it was random."

"It wasn't," I said.

I didn't want to tell her any details about how I knew that. I wasn't sure what Tucker would or wouldn't be making public yet, and as much as I wanted this information, I wasn't about to get in the way of an official investigation to get it. I hurried on before she could push for more details.

"Her name was Summer Martin," I said.

Margene sucked in a breath that made a whistling sound.

"Oh, Emma. How long have you got? I barely know anyone who's had to work with that woman who doesn't hate her. I mean, not her clients. As I'm sure you'll know having worked with her, she's a dream for her clients. But all of her contacts put up with her simply because they have no real choice if they want to cater the bigger weddings."

"That's kind of what I thought," I admitted. "I just wondered if you knew of anyone who might have more of a reason than simply not liking her attitude. Like you said, murder is a bit extreme for someone who has only been on the end of one of Summer's tongue lashings."

"Hmm, that's true," Margene said. "Let me think. There's Hilary Button, but she left town years ago and I really can't see her re-surfacing now to exact revenge on a years old grudge. And then there's Doris Young."

My heart started to race at the mention of Doris. I didn't want to seem too eager so I just waited, resisting the urge to demand that Margene tell me everything.

"I can't see Doris as a murderer. She's a no nonsense type, a nice enough woman. But it's not like she doesn't have a motive. Summer cheated her out of a payment for the floral arrangements for a wedding a couple of years ago. Summer claimed the flowers weren't right, that they were the wrong ones. The bride was happy with them; she said they were correct, but Summer insisted they were wrong and Doris never did get the money for them. She was cheated out of thousands of dollars and she never really got over it. I hear she makes Summer pay upfront now. Or rather, she did."

It sounded like a more solid motive than what I had for Derrick and I quickly added it to my notes.

"Can you think of anyone else?" I asked.

"No," Margene said. "Not anyone who has a better reason than a strong dislike for the woman, and if you want to know about that, then you'll have a list as long as your arm. But you can relax anyway, honey. If Doris finally decided to get her own back on Summer for cheating her, then she's most certainly not going to be a problem at your wedding."

"That's a relief, at least," I said.

"Oh, and if you speak to anyone else about this and they mention the name Derrick Williams, ignore them," she added.

"Why?" I asked, interested to get her take on the whole Derrick situation without having to bring it up myself. "He's my photographer. Should I be worried?"

"Not even a little bit," Margene said. "People often accuse him of things because he has an old criminal record. But I know all the parties involved and, honestly, it was all a misunderstanding, if you ask me."

"So you believe he's harmless?" I asked, needing to hear her clarify it.

"In my opinion. He was never the villain he was made out to be. I hope that's put your mind at rest, Emma," Margene said.

"It has. Thank you, Margene. I have to ask for one more favor, though," I said.

"Go on," Margene urged me.

"Please don't tell my grandma I called you. She'll only worry if she thinks I'm worried, and you know how she gets. She'd never believe I'm not upset, and I don't want this to spoil the wedding for her."

"Don't worry, dear. I completely understand," Margene said. "My lips are sealed."

I seriously doubted that was true, but Margene and my grandma were good friends, and I knew that as much as Margene enjoyed a good gossip, she would leave my name out of it as she wouldn't want to upset my grandma. She would just talk, not mentioning any names, and my grandma would soak all the gossip up, never bothering to question its source.

I thanked Margene again and hung up the call. It was starting to look more likely that Doris Young was my chief suspect. I wasn't quite ready to rule Derrick out altogether just yet, but Margene had defended him and she was usually a good judge of character.

6

I was filled with nervous energy again, but this time, there was no excitement. I wasn't nervous about the wedding, at least not for now. No, I was nervous about the wedding planner, or more accurately, her death and who had caused it.

As much as I had liked Doris Young, it was looking more and more likely that she was the culprit. A couple of thousand dollars, Summer getting one over on her, Summer's attitude towards her... It all added up to a good motive, a simmering resentment that had finally come to the surface and boiled over. It seemed to make more sense than Derrick as a suspect. I had to know more, though. I had to be sure before I could call Tucker and tell him who had killed Summer and why. And as of yet, all I had was an assumption. I needed concrete proof.

But where was I meant to find that? I knew I could call Doris and ask to go down to Flower Power under the pretence that I wanted to see something or ask something. I would have to be super careful, however. If Doris suspected I was on to her, what was to stop her killing me? And I'd already given her a head's up that I wasn't above lying about wanting to see something if there was something to gain from it. I cursed myself for asking to see a bouquet similar in size to mine the other day, just to get rid of the moment of awkwardness between Doris and Summer. It would have been an ideal cover story for now, the perfect way to get into the back of the store and potentially be left alone to dig around for clues.

There was another option, of course. It wasn't one I relished the thought of, but I knew it could be the difference between me finding some evidence to back up my theory or not finding anything at all. And until I knew for sure, I really couldn't rule Derrick, or indeed half of Hillbilly Hollow, out of this.

With a sigh, I closed my laptop and headed for the stairs. Trailed by Snowball, I went to the kitchen, where the little goat instantly ran for one of my grandma's tea towels. My grandma saw her coming and moved the towel from her reach, laughing at her indignant bleat.

"I have to go out for awhile. I won't be long," I said.

"You're getting involved again, aren't you?" Grandma asked.

I raised an eyebrow. How did she know?

"Margene called," Grandma said. She laughed at my expression. "Oh, don't worry, she kept your secret. She just said she'd heard that Summer had been killed and then launched into a long discussion about who it could have been. I didn't put it together at first, but now you're rushing off somewhere in such a hurry that you've forgotten you don't have any shoes on. And after you told me you had a lot of work to get through? I can put two and two together, you know."

I looked down at my feet and saw that Grandma was right. I had indeed forgotten to put my shoes on. I knew there was no point in trying to deny it now, so I nodded sheepishly.

Grandma sighed. "I'm not going to try to tell you to stay out of it, Emma, because I know you won't. But I am going to ask two things of you. Firstly, please be careful. I've lost count of the times you've almost been killed because of one of these investigations."

"I'll be careful," I promised. "I'm only going to see Autumn. I'm not going after anyone dangerous. At least, not yet."

Grandma raised her eyebrow at the last part, but she made no comment.

"The second thing is not to let this take over. You're two days away from your wedding, Emma. You're meant to be enjoying this time. Don't let this whole thing ruin your wedding day for you and Billy, okay? I know it's only one day, and you're starting a life together based on more than that, but it's a day you'll both remember forever, and I want you to remember it for the right reasons."

"I promise you this won't ruin the wedding. I won't let it," I said. "I want so badly for our day to be perfect."

"Off you go, then. I can see you're dying to," Grandma said.

I smiled my thanks at her and said goodbye. I was almost at the front door when she ran out of the kitchen behind me.

"Emma?" she said.

I turned back reluctantly, already dreading this part. The part where she begged me not to go and I had to go anyway.

"Your shoes." She smiled.

I was relieved she wasn't trying to talk me out of it, and annoyed at myself for forgetting my shoes yet again.

"Thanks Grandma. I swear this wedding planning has got me a mess. Imagine what I would have been like if Billy and I had tried to do all of this alone."

"I dread to think." Grandma laughed.

I ran up to the attic and pushed my feet into my sneakers. Then I hurried back down the stairs and straight out the front door before I could change my mind or get called back for anything else.

I jumped in the truck, put it into drive and headed out for Summer's office building. Now I just had to hope that Autumn was there. And that she was willing to let me poke around in her dead sister's things. I felt bad for disturbing Autumn at this time, but it was Summer herself who had pushed me to get involved. It wasn't like I was just being nosey.

I PUSHED on the door to Summer's office unit and smiled to myself when it opened. At least one thing had gone right today. Stepping inside, I closed the door quietly behind me. The place began with a small lobby with a desk and chair for a receptionist and two small chairs and a coffee table adorned with bridal magazines. I presumed it was a waiting area. Judging by the empty feel to the place, Summer and now Autumn didn't bank on receiving many visitors here. Now I thought about it, I had never been here. We always met at the farm, or at Billy's house or at one venue or another.

No one manned the desk and no one appeared to be coming from anywhere to see who I was or why I was here. Maybe I wouldn't even have to disturb Autumn. Maybe I could just sneak into Summer's office myself and have a look around. If I found something, then surely Autumn would just be grateful that I had helped to solve her sister's murder. And if I didn't, well she would never have to know I had even been here.

I wondered briefly if Tucker had already been here and searched Summer's office, but I dismissed the idea. He wouldn't have thought to come to this place. He would no doubt have searched her house, but knowing Summer and how her business was her life, I suspected anything of significance would be right here on her business premises.

I looked around quickly. A fire exit stood to my left and a passageway snaked off to my right. Wherever Summer's private office was, it had to be down that passageway. I began to walk along it, staying as silent as I could. The doors were solid, no glass, which made me happy. There was no risk of Autumn or whoever was here glancing up from their desk at the wrong moment and spotting me creeping past.

I moved quickly, passing a door marked *Autumn Martin*. I practically held my breath as I made my way past. The door opposite it read *Supplies*. A few more bore no name plates. The one at the end bore the name I was looking for. *Summer Martin.* I reached out, preparing to open the door. As my hand touched the handle, I heard a noise behind me and I turned to find Autumn standing there, an eyebrow raised. She held herself tall, and for the first time since I had met her, she looked confident.

"And what exactly do you think you're doing going in there?" she asked, her voice low and menacing.

I had two choices. I could be honest with her and hope she took pity on me and wanted her sister's murder solved. Or I could lie. There was only one problem with my second plan. In the moment, caught out like that, I couldn't think of any lie that was even vaguely convincing.

As I tried to decide what to say, I noticed a change in Autumn. Her shoulders slumped, her posture returning to normal. She sighed loudly and when she spoke again, there was no menace in her tone, only a deflated acceptance.

"It's okay," she said. "I know why you're here. You only pretended you were going to let me take over your wedding planning on the phone because you were too polite to say no. So you sneaked over here to steal your file and check up on me, didn't you? Were you planning on firing me straight away or would you at least have waited until I actually deserved it?"

I felt awful looking at Autumn's face. She wore an expression that said she had been expecting this. She had really left me no choice here. I had to tell her the truth. It was bad enough that she had lost her sister. I didn't want her to think she might lose her business as well. Not because of me.

"I can explain," I said.

Autumn shrugged. "You don't need to explain. I'm no Summer, I get that. But I need you to know I'm not useless, Emma. I'm just quieter than Summer, but my way works as well as hers, maybe more so because none of the vendors hate me."

She went quiet, aware of what she'd said. I made no comment on it and she went on.

"You can have your file. I just wish you had been honest with me. You won't find the file in there, though."

"Listen to me, Autumn. I'm not firing you. Assuming you still want to work with me after what I'm about to tell you," I said. "Can we go into your office to talk about this?"

"Sure," Autumn said, looking curious.

At least she was willing to hear me out. That was something. She turned and went into her office. I followed her, shutting the door behind me. She motioned for me to sit down. I took the chair she indicated and took a deep breath. Then I told her the truth.

"What I'm about to say stays in this room," I started.

Autumn nodded her understanding.

"I don't know how well you know Sheriff Tucker, but ..."

"I've known him for years," Autumn interrupted me.

"So you'll know he's a nice person but he....struggles a bit in his job, yes?"

She smiled a little and nodded again. "That's true but he tries, doesn't he? Like he genuinely cares about the people in Hillbilly Hollow," she said.

"Oh yes, that he does. But his strong point isn't as a

detective. In the past, I've found myself being kind of an amateur sleuth and helping to nudge the police in the right direction. Summer was good to me, and... I don't know. I just kind of feel like I owe her one. I wasn't going into her office for my file. I was going in there to see if I could find any clues at all to the identity of her murderer."

"Wow," Autumn breathed. "I have to admit I didn't see that one coming. Are you serious?"

I nodded.

"Tell me the truth, Emma, because your file really is in here."

"I'm telling you the truth. I would have asked your permission, but I know her death is still so fresh and I didn't want to upset you when it could be for nothing. I figured if I didn't find anything, then you wouldn't have to be reminded of what had happened."

I was telling the truth. Or almost the truth. I wasn't about to explain that her sister's ghost had threatened to ruin my honeymoon if I didn't find her killer. That would be the point where Autumn either thought I was crazy or lying to her.

As if reading my mind, she said, "How can I forget her death? I feel like her ghost is here watching me. Does that sound crazy?"

Not to me. How could it?

I shook my head. "No," I said. "I think it's normal to feel like someone is still watching over you, even if you think they're only watching to make sure you don't mess anything up."

She smiled at the last part and shook her head. "Okay.

So here's the thing. I can't bring myself to go into Summer's office so soon. Luckily the files are kept in a common area so I haven't had to go in to get anyone's information yet. But I don't mind if you do."

"You're sure?" I checked.

"I'm sure," she confirmed. "Hey if you can solve this thing, then who am I to stop you?"

"Thanks," I said. "I'll let you know when I'm done."

I left her office and walked back along the hallway to Summer's office. I felt nervous suddenly, like I was invading Summer's privacy by going into her office alone. I reminded myself once more that this investigation was being done at her request, as I pushed the door open and stepped inside.

The office was exactly what I would have expected from Summer, immaculate and modern looking. Nothing sat on her desk except for a computer. The books on the shelves that lined the far wall were organized alphabetically. Everything about the office screamed efficiency.

As I looked across the titles on the bookshelf, my mind went back to Autumn. She had been helpful, but she was almost too helpful. I wondered if there was anything suspicious in that. After all, she had every motive to kill Summer. Summer always treated her badly, perhaps worse than she treated any of her contacts, and it would have been incessant for Autumn, who had to be around her all day every day.

But then I shook my head. Could someone really be too helpful when it came to something like this? Maybe she was being helpful because she really thought I could solve this murder. She knew Tucker. That meant she had to know that I was her best shot at solving this, even if she didn't know my reputation, which she didn't seem to.

I moved away from the book shelf. Nothing looked to be out of place and I didn't want to waste my time looking through the wrong space. I knew where I should be searching, I was just reluctant to poke through Summer's personal correspondence. I told myself I was just being silly and made my way over to her desk.

I sat down in the chair and opened the top drawer. Rifling through the papers there, I found that they were all invoices and receipts. The next drawer down held stationery supplies and business cards, both hers and ones for contacts she had picked up along the way, all held together in a sleek organizer. I didn't bother checking, but I would have been willing to bet every cent I had that they too were alphabetized.

The bottom drawer was empty except for a few sheets of paper. The logo on the letterhead was Flower Power's logo and I took them to be more invoices. I started to shut the drawer, but a voice in the back of my mind whispered to me, asking if I really thought Summer was the type to not have all of her invoices together.

Maybe this was the invoice for the job Summer had swindled Doris on, the one Margene had told me about? It wouldn't be concrete proof of anything, but it could be useful to at least see it.

I lifted the papers out and began to flick through them. My eyebrows rose as I read each of the three sheets. They were all threatening letters from Doris to Summer, claiming that one day Doris would have her revenge. The notes said that Summer had better watch her back or she could find herself coming to a bad end.

My heart hammered in my chest. This could be it. This could be the evidence that Doris was guilty of Summer's murder. It wasn't enough to go on alone, but it was definitely compelling proof of Doris's total hatred for Summer, more compelling than town gossip ever could be. And it was solid, something tangible that showed Doris had a motive for the murder. Now if I could just find one more thing to tie Doris directly to the killing this could well be over.

I wondered for a moment how I could find more on Doris. I should probably hand these letters over to Tucker and wash my hands of this, but Tucker would say what I already knew; sending someone a threatening letter and actually murdering them weren't the same thing. No, I needed more.

I had to find a way to get into Doris's home and search it while she was at work. Then maybe I could find the incriminating tool she had used to cut the brake lines. Or I might find a manual or something detailing how to do it. I didn't know exactly what the proof would be, but I had to find something.

I also knew it would likely have to wait until Billy and I came back from our honeymoon. The shop would be closed for the day now, and I certainly didn't want to interrupt Doris tomorrow. She would be working on our wedding flowers.

As much as it pained me to admit I would put this off to get my flowers, I would. There was no way I could get another florist on such notice, and I didn't think for a second Doris was dangerous to any of my guests. It wasn't like she would be at the wedding itself like Derrick.

I slipped the notes into my pocket and left Summer's office. I tapped on Autumn's door on the way past.

"Come in," she called.

I pushed the door open.

"I'm just letting you know I'm leaving," I said.

"Okay," she agreed. "Now stop worrying about this and get some rest before your big day."

I nodded. She looked away and then back up at me.

"Did ... did you find anything?" she asked.

"Nothing I can use on its own, but maybe something that will point me in the right direction. That's really all I can say right now," I said awkwardly.

Autumn nodded. "It's okay. I understand," she said.

I left the building wondering if Autumn was really alright. She seemed so detached from the whole thing, like it was happening to someone else. I reminded myself that she was probably still in shock. It would all hit her soon enough.

I went to my truck and drove back to the farm, conscious of how late it was getting and how much work I had to get through tonight. And that was without thinking about the murder and what exactly those notes proved or didn't prove.

7

It was the night of the rehearsal dinner. The rehearsal itself had gone perfectly well, and it had been easy for me to imagine how perfect Hope Community would look with the floral arrangements in place, how perfect we would all look in our wedding clothes.

The black cocktail dress I had chosen for tonight was nice enough, but it didn't compare to my wedding dress. Billy looked resplendent in his black suit, but I knew he would look even better tomorrow at the wedding.

I couldn't believe it was finally nearly time. After so long resisting Billy's charms, and then what felt like the world's longest engagement, we were finally here, ready to take our vows.

Just one more night. That was all that kept going through my head. One more night as a single woman. Suzy had been quick to remind me that I should embrace every moment of my single life, although it was hard to believe she meant it. She was positively glowing since marrying Brian and having Emma Rose.

I'd opted against having a night out with the girls. Instead, Suzy, Beth and I had spent a pleasant few hours having brunch together this morning before the rehearsal got underway. It was nice, just chatting with my friends and enjoying the most delicious pancakes I had ever tasted.

I didn't regret my decision for a moment. My evening was busy enough after the rehearsal and soon I meant to get an early start on a full night's sleep.

I looked around the dinner table. My grandparents were there, of course. Suzy and Brian were there with little Emma Rose. Brian was Billy's best man and naturally Suzy was my matron of honor. The other three groomsmen were at the rehearsal dinner too; Billy's two brothers and an old friend from medical school. And Beth, my only other bridesmaid. They were the people who mattered most to me. There would be more people at the wedding. We'd invited what felt like the whole town, but these were our nearest and dearest.

"Are you alright?" Billy asked me quietly as we ate our meal.

The meal was beautiful. Chicken in a creamy mushroom sauce with sautéed potatoes and a cauliflower puree.

"I'm fine." I smiled at him.

"You seem quiet," he said. He laughed nervously. "You're not having second thoughts, are you?"

"Never," I reassured him. "I was actually just thinking that the people in this room are the most important people in the world to us. It seems so magical to have them all here in one place to share this with, doesn't it?"

"It does." Billy smiled. "But just remember, there's another person in the room too."

I frowned, not understanding what he meant. He laughed softly at my expression and nodded to Derrick. Derrick was here in an official capacity, taking pictures of the rehearsal for our wedding album.

"Just try not to look like you'd rather be somewhere else." Billy laughed. "I'm not sure that's a look we want to try to explain to our grandkids one day."

I laughed and nodded, melting inside at the thought of us growing old together and one day having grandkids to share our memories with. It felt so far away, and yet, I knew how fast time passed us by and it would be here before we knew it. The notion made me even more determined to enjoy every minute of tonight and tomorrow. One day, this weekend would be a distant memory, and when that happened, I wanted it to be a good one.

As we finished up the meal, the wait staff quietly moved in and cleared the plates, replacing them with a delicious looking slice of pie. As I ate it, trying to concentrate on the conversations and laughter around me, I couldn't help but find myself watching Derrick. Margene had mostly reassured me that he was harmless, but I kept thinking what if she was wrong? What if she had believed the wrong story?

Derrick's sullen expression as he moved among the tables snapping pictures did nothing to quell my anxiety. Was he always like this? I had no idea. I had never met the man before my wedding planning began. Maybe it was his way of trying to blend into the background and be unobtrusive. Maybe he was upset about Summer's death and was just doing his best to get through the night. Or maybe he was planning his next kill. Maybe he was going to strike at my wedding.

I told myself my last thought was ridiculous. Even if Derrick had killed Summer, in his mind, he had a reason for it. There was a difference between some sort of revenge killing and picking off random people at a wedding. Still, the idea that I might have a murderer present at my wedding did nothing to keep me focused on the moment.

I shook my head, trying to shake away the worries. Deep down, although I wasn't ready to rule Derrick out completely quite yet, I didn't really believe he had done it. He was maybe just one of those people who hated their jobs and did nothing at all to try and hide that fact, not even from paying customers.

I still thought Doris was the best suspect for Summer's murder. She had more than enough motive. Not only did Summer treat her with obvious distain, she had also robbed the woman of a fair chunk of money. And then there were the threatening notes. Those alone didn't prove Doris had done anything wrong. Sending a nasty note and murdering someone were worlds apart. But it put her at the very top of my suspect list. She had expressed murderous thoughts, which was more than Derrick had done. At least Doris wouldn't actually be present at the wedding once the guests started to arrive.

"Come on, Suzy, surely it's time for your speech now,"

Richard, one of Billy's brothers, said as we finished up the dessert.

"Oh no, no one wants to hear from me." Suzy laughed.

She made it clear that her protest was only a formality. It was obvious to me that she very much wanted to give a speech. I smiled to myself as Richard waved away her protest and Suzy got to her feet.

"Well, what can I say about Emma?" she began.

She had obviously put a lot of thought into the speech. That was just Suzy's way. I wondered briefly what she would have done if no one had requested it. It honestly wouldn't have surprised me all that much to learn that she had put Richard up to his request, prior to the dinner.

"Emma is my best friend. We've been best friends since we met on the first day of elementary school and we've never looked back. We've been through it all together: our first holidays, our first loves, our first heartbreaks. We've laughed and cried and shared our secrets. And when I married Brian, Emma was right there by my side, as I will be there for her tomorrow. I named my daughter after Emma, which I think tells all you need to know about how much I love this girl. I just hope my own little Emma turns out to be every bit as smart, funny, and utterly amazing as my best friend."

She paused and raised her glass.

"Here's to you, Emma, my best friend, and to Billy, the man who will spend the rest of his life making Emma happy, or he'll have me to answer to."

Laughter came at that and Billy did a theatrical gulp.

"I guess I'd better be good to you then, huh?" he teased me.

Suzy sipped from her glass.

"To Emma and Billy," she said.

"To Emma and Billy," the guests repeated.

I could feel my cheeks flushing from the champagne and the embarrassment of having all eyes on me. That was the one part of my wedding I was really dreading. Being the center of attention was always more Suzy's thing than mine. I was happier as part of the crowd.

Suzy sat back down, smiling as the guests clapped their hands for her. I wished she could walk down the aisle in my place and I could just pop up from somewhere behind the altar to recite my vows.

I was pulled out of my worries as Derrick approached and took a few group shots of Billy and me with various members of the party. By the time he had finished, I had managed to pretty much swallow down my worries about walking down the aisle, but that left room in my head for my doubts about Derrick to creep back in.

I reminded myself about the whole innocent until proven guilty thing and turned my focus back to Doris. Maybe I could slip into her home tomorrow while I knew she would be distracted at the church. I dismissed the idea immediately. Billy would never forgive me if I was late to our wedding because of me snooping around in Summer's murder investigation. I still hadn't told him I was looking into it at all, or about her ghostly visit and the threat of ruining our honeymoon. Besides, I told myself, everyone needs a day off, even those seeking justice for ghostly visitors.

As Derrick moved around the room, my gaze followed him, and out of the corner of my eye, I spotted Autumn. She had hung back, keeping herself scarce, staying behind the scenes and making sure everything was running according to plan. What had happened to draw her out?

I didn't think I could handle any more bad news. She was having what looked to be a very heated discussion with the head caterer. She seemed pretty nervous. Was she regretting taking on my wedding? Was the whole thing too much for her in the wake of her sister's death?

It looked like she was on the verge of cracking under the pressure of holding together such a big event for the first time by herself. Was that why she was nervous? Had something gone wrong with tomorrow's catering? Or did she have darker reasons to be uneasy? Was she trying to cover up a crime she had a pretty good motive for?

"Would you excuse me for a moment?" I said politely to the table.

Whatever was going on, now that I had seen how worried Autumn looked, I could feel the nerves myself. I wouldn't be able to relax and enjoy the evening until I knew exactly what was going on.

I stood up and casually made my way over to Autumn and the caterer. Autumn saw me approaching and smiled warmly at me.

"Hi Emma. Is everything okay? Are you enjoying yourself?" she asked.

"Everything's perfect," I assured her. "The meal was delicious."

She waited, smiling questioningly at me. She clearly knew there had to be a reason I had wandered over here.

"I just ... I couldn't help but notice the conversation you two were having and how stressed you look, Autumn," I said.

Autumn shook her head and frowned slightly. "That's nothing for you to worry about," she said.

"But there is. Look, if something's wrong I'd rather know now and at least attempt to help fix it rather than find out tomorrow when it's too late to do anything about it," I said.

"Would you have said that to Summer? Or would you have trusted her to handle it?" Autumn asked me.

I felt myself blush at her probing question. No doubt if Summer were here, I would have been equally worried, but I probably wouldn't have come over here. I would have trusted her to deal with the problem herself. I decided to tell Autumn a half truth, one I hoped would take the sting out of my obvious lack of faith in her.

"If the situation was reversed and Summer was here, having lost her sister earlier in the week, yes, I would have said the same thing to her," I replied. "Otherwise, I would have trusted her to fix it. Just like in different circumstances I would have trusted you to fix it."

The different circumstances being if I didn't half suspect her of somehow being involved in her sister's murder. I kept that thought to myself.

Autumn smiled at me, some of the anger leaving her.

"I assure you that I am handling this, Emma. I did lose my sister, but in some ways that's what is keeping me going. I know if it was the other way around, Summer wouldn't have crumbled. She'd have bulldozed her way through your plans and made sure this was the wedding of the year. And that's exactly what I'm going to do. Now I'll tell you what's going on, but only because I think it will put your mind at rest, not because I need you to step in and do my job for me. Okay?"

I nodded and Autumn returned the nod.

"There is absolutely nothing wrong for tomorrow. Everything is on track and I am one thousand percent confident nothing will go wrong. I am a little stressed tonight, but it's nothing major. I guess I'm affected by Summer's death more than I care to admit, because I did snap at the catering manager. There is a slight delay getting the coffee course out because the boilers are taking a little longer than normal to heat up. That's it."

I felt relief flood me. It was nothing. Something a wedding planner would worry about because precision timing was totally their deal, but not something I needed to worry about. Not something I even would have noticed under ordinary circumstances when I wasn't watching every little thing and viewing everyone as a potential murder suspect.

Autumn turned to the catering manager.

"Please accept my apologies for my overreaction. I guess maybe I'm channelling my inner Summer a little too much."

"It's fine." The catering manager smiled. "Trust me, you're a whole lot easier to work with than Summer ever was. She probably would have fired me for this."

Another suspect? No, I had to stop thinking this way at my rehearsal dinner. I didn't want to look back on this day and remember nothing except details of the investigation.

Autumn turned back to me.

"Now, you go back to that handsome fiancé of yours and enjoy your night, Emma. You have nothing to worry about, I promise you."

"Thank you. And I'm sorry for being so overbearing."

Autumn laughed. "Trust me, I've worked with some real bridezillas over the years. You are a delight to work with."

I returned to my seat, sure that Autumn was telling me the truth. Everything was fine. And I was becoming more and more convinced that she wasn't the one to have killed Summer. She was just doing what she said she was doing, throwing herself into her work to take her mind off what had happened. It made sense. It was pretty much how I thought I would react in the same circumstances if I was her. Except I would probably have a ghostly version of my dead relative on my case.

"Is everything alright?" Billy asked when I sat back down. "I saw you talking to Autumn."

"Everything's fine," I said. "There's a bit of a delay with the coffee, that's all."

"Autumn looks a bit stressed out, doesn't she?" Billy asked. "I feel kind of bad having her keep working on the wedding after what's happened."

"Me too," I agreed. "But she insisted. She says working is taking her mind off Summer, and I get that."

The conversation was cut short as music filled the air and Suzy grabbed my arm and pulled me to my feet.

"Sorry Billy, I need to borrow Emma for a while," she said.

Billy laughed and gestured for her to take me. I laughingly followed Suzy towards the dance floor as music began pumping out of the speakers.

"What the ...?" I said.

"Surprise." Suzy grinned. "I get why you didn't want a girls night, but that doesn't mean you get out of dancing the night away with me."

I laughed. "What if other people come to the restaurant?" I said.

"They won't." Suzy winked. "I gave Mrs. Harris a nice fat gift voucher for my store in exchange for making tonight a private party."

I shook my head, not knowing what to say.

Suzy read my expression. "You don't have to say anything. You just have to dance," she said.

She took my hand and spun me around and I laughed. The rest of the night passed by in a blur of happy moments, laughing and dancing. We did eventually get our coffees, and for a few hours I was able to forget all about Summer Martin and her murderer.

8

After a long but fun-filled evening, I was finally back home at the farmhouse. Billy and I had said our goodbyes after he dropped me off, and we had of course agreed that we wouldn't see each other now until the actual wedding. Our wedding planner being murdered a few days before our wedding was surely bad enough luck. We certainly didn't want to invite any more by breaking a tradition as old as this one.

My grandparents had just turned in. I sat at the kitchen table sipping the last of my cup of hot chocolate with Snowball sitting between my feet, her head resting on my lap. I absently stroked her ear and the top of her head, thinking how this would be my last night officially living here on the farm before I moved in with Billy.

It was surreal, but it felt right. It was time to start the next chapter of my life. I drained the last of my hot chocolate and went to the sink. I washed my cup out, dried it and put it away. I didn't want to leave any mess behind for tomorrow.

I decided it was time to call it a night. It was only eleven, but I wanted a good night's sleep so I was as fresh as possible in the morning. I headed for the back door so I could go and use the outhouse before bed. Snowball walked at my side.

"This is one thing I won't miss," I said quietly to her as we walked. "It'll be lovely to have indoor plumbing, especially in the winter when it's freezing cold out here."

She bleated in response, and I took it as agreement. I reached the outhouse and used the toilet. Snowball was waiting patiently for me on the other side of the door as I came back out.

"Come on girl, let's go back inside and you can enjoy your last night curled up on my bed," I said.

As we headed back to the house, Snowball moved away from me suddenly and lay down on the ground. I felt a sinking feeling in my stomach. Whenever she did that, it usually meant I was about to get a visitor from beyond the grave. Seeing Summer and getting another lecture from her was the last thing I needed right now. I sighed loudly and waited for her to put in an appearance.

I didn't have to wait long, but her visit this time was even briefer than the last. She appeared in the distance, an ethereal figure in white who floated above the ground for a few seconds and then vanished. There was no following me around or talking to me, so I figured she must approve of what I had discovered so far.

Either that, or this was just a brief warning that she was back and would be next to me in seconds. I felt a shiver go down my spine at the thought of it, but I dismissed the idea when Snowball returned to my side. That had to mean Summer was gone again for now.

I headed quickly back into the kitchen and slammed the door closed behind me, narrowly missing Snowball's tail. I knew that according to all of the stories ghosts could walk through walls like they weren't there and a closed door was unlikely to keep Summer out if she wanted to follow me to my room, but I still felt better for shutting the door.

I made my way up to my attic room, trailed by Snowball, and changed into my night clothes. After sitting down in front of my small dresser, I removed my make-up and brushed my hair out before putting a thin layer of moisturizer on. There. I was prepared for tomorrow. Or at least my skin was.

I turned the light out and slipped into bed quickly before I could think of anything else I needed to do. Everything would have to wait until after the wedding now, until after Billy and I had returned from our honeymoon. Anything I may have forgotten would just have to stay forgotten.

Still, my thoughts kept going back to Derrick and Doris and the threatening letters. There was something there niggling at the edge of my mind, but I couldn't quite grasp what it was. The more I tried to focus on it, the further away it seemed to slip. I tried clearing my mind and letting it come, but it was no good. The less I tried to think about it, the more prevalent it was in my thoughts. I knew it would come to me eventually, and when it did I would most likely kick myself that it had taken me so long, but something told me that wouldn't happen tonight. I had enough worries about my wedding tomorrow without trying to chase vague theories and suspicions.

I forced myself to close my eyes and think of nothing but my wedding. The investigation would have to wait now. I certainly wasn't going to be doing any investigating on my wedding day. Like everything else, it would get done when I got back from our honeymoon, and if Summer didn't like that, then quite frankly, she could lump it. Tomorrow would be the start of my new life, and I didn't want my last night here at my grandparents' house to be tainted with thoughts of murder and troublesome ghosts.

As I slipped into sleep, my last thought was of how handsome Billy was going to look in his suit tomorrow, and I figured that was exactly the kind of thing I should actually be thinking about tonight.

9

My stomach was roiling with nerves as I stepped out of the car in front of Hope Community Church. Suzy, Beth and my grandpa quickly followed behind me. Suzy and Beth moved around me, arranging my dress.

I looked down at myself when they had finished. My white dress had a tight bodice and no straps or sleeves. From my waist, it flowed, a beautiful cascade of white netting. Silver details on the bodice caught the sunlight and made it look like I was sparkling.

Suzy had done my hair and make-up this morning. My eyes were smoky, my lips and cheeks pink. I wore the front part of my hair pinned back, the length of it tumbling down my back in loose curls. My veil was pinned in place.

Suzy took both of my hands in hers and smiled at me.

"Don't be nervous, Emma. You look gorgeous, and everything is going to be just fine," she said.

I smiled back at her, hardly daring to speak in case I

burst into tears and ruined my make-up. Beth handed me my bouquet, and between the two of them, they covered my face with my veil. They walked on ahead, leaving me and my grandpa alone for a moment.

"This is it, Emma. Your last chance to run," Grandpa said.

"Oh, I missed that opportunity when I put these shoes on." I laughed.

I nodded down towards my feet, clad in white satin shoes with heels so big I felt like I would go tumbling over at any second. I clung to my grandpa's arm for dear life.

"Seriously, Emma. Billy is a good man," Grandpa said.

"Is that your way of saying you approve of him?" I smiled.

"Yes, I think maybe it is." He grinned back. "I just hope that one day you two get to the ages Dorothy and I are now, and you're both still as much in love as we are."

I fanned my face frantically with my hands as tears prickled in the corners of my eyes.

"Oh Grandpa, don't. I can't cry yet. I want to at least look half decent as I walk down the aisle," I exclaimed.

"You look more than half decent, Emma. You look stunning," he said, his voice filled with pride.

I was glad to reach the doors to Hope Community and have Suzy and Beth join us again, otherwise I was certain I would have lost the battle with my tears.

Suzy and Beth moved behind me, picking up my train. Grandpa raised a questioning eyebrow at me, asking if I was ready, and I nodded. I was definitely ready to become Mrs. Stone.

We entered the church and I instantly heard the wedding march start up on the organ. Billy and I had opted for the traditional song for me to walk down the aisle to. I clung even more tightly to my grandpa as we moved slowly along the aisle. I could feel the heat rising to my cheeks, partly from nervousness at knowing all eyes were on me, and partly from excitement. I still could hardly believe that my wedding was finally here.

I glanced to my left and my right as I walked. The flowers really did pop, and the arch up ahead looked exactly how I had imagined it would. Stunning. Looking at the flowers, their beauty, the work that had gone into every little detail of the arrangements, it was hard to imagine Doris Young as a murderer. I scolded myself, telling myself now was most definitely not the time to be thinking about that.

After what felt like a lifetime, I finally reached the altar and Billy. He looked every bit as handsome as I had imagined he would in his grey suit and light pink shirt. He smiled as I approached him and I smiled back, feeling my eyes twinkling with emotion.

Grandpa placed my hand into Billy's and then went and took his seat beside Grandma, who was looking very elegant in her Sunday best. Billy squeezed my hand and then released it to push my veil back as Suzy and Beth took their places behind me.

The pastor smiled at us warmly and began the ceremony. Our vows flew by without a hitch. I didn't stutter or splutter or, worse, get Billy's name wrong, all of which I had done in my worst nightmares in the weeks leading up to the wedding.

"You may kiss the bride," the pastor finally announced.

I felt a swirl of excitement in my stomach as Billy leaned down and our lips touched. Sparks seemed to fly and I was momentarily taken aback by the reminder of how much I loved this man.

The pastor finished off the ceremony and Billy and I signed the register, along with our witnesses. We left the church, followed by our wedding party, now Dr. and Mrs. Stone.

The guests began to disperse, headed for the reception, as Billy and I and our bridesmaids and groomsmen stood uncertainly in the doorway, waiting to see what would happen next. My grandparents had taken Emma Rose and I knew it wouldn't be too long before Suzy began getting a little anxious without her here with us.

Derrick appeared as if from nowhere and began organizing us into groups and poses around the flower beds at the front of the church. I remembered Summer saying he would check for the places with the best lighting and views, and I had to admit he had chosen spectacularly. While I might have had my misgivings about Derrick last night, today he was like a different person. He was happy, smiling and shouting cheerful instructions to us all. I let myself relax. Obviously he had just been having an off night last night. It happened to us all sometimes.

Once Derrick had taken a huge number of photos, Autumn appeared, smiling brightly at us.

"Congratulations, Dr. and Mrs. Stone." She beamed.

My face flushed as she called me by my new name. It would take some getting used to, but I liked it.

"Thank you," we said in unison and everyone laughed.

"Oh no," Suzy groaned jokingly. "They'll be finishing each other's sentences by next week."

Autumn laughed and then turned back to me.

"Emma, Billy, Suzy and Brian, you have a few more shots left to do. If the rest of you would like to come with me, I'll drive you over to the reception," she said.

I said a quick goodbye and thank you to Beth, and Billy shook hands with his groomsmen and then they were whisked away by Autumn, who was wearing a yellow sundress with a wide brown belt. I smiled to myself as I watched her walk away, her hair its usually frizzy tangle. I had half expected her to show up looking like Summer would have. I was glad she hadn't; it would have been too weird.

Once Autumn had taken the others away, Derrick took us around the back of the church, to the beautiful waterfall. I had forgotten that Billy hadn't yet seen the little oasis.

"You weren't kidding about how this place was the perfect venue, were you?" he whispered.

I shook my head. "Nope."

"And you are the perfect bride. But I always knew you would be," he added.

He kissed my cheek and Derrick's flash went off as he caught the moment. I had a feeling that photo was going to be my favorite picture out of all of them. It was natural rather than posed and it had the stunning waterfall in the background.

Fifteen minutes and what felt like a hundred more

photos later, we were done. Derrick headed for his car, telling us our car was on its way. We waited for a minute or two and a large silver limousine appeared. I frowned and glanced at Billy. We hadn't ordered this. The driver got out and came to open the doors.

"Hi," I said. "I think there might have been some mistake. We ..."

"All part of the service, ma'am," he said smiling. "Autumn's special touch."

We exchanged glances again and I felt my face breaking into a wide smile.

"It's perfect. Just enjoy it," Suzy said, laughing as we got in. "I can't believe you were trying to talk us out of this."

We sat in the limousine sipping champagne on the short drive to my grandparents' house. The reception was being held in their backyard. My grandpa had even moved some of the cows from the field next to the yard and paid a couple of local kids to remove all the cow pats so we could have the extra space for the day. It was the outdoor country reception Billy and I had dreamed of.

I had yet to see the place decorated. Autumn's team had waited to come in until after I had left that morning. We pulled up at the front of the house and got out, thanking the driver, who tipped his hat and congratulated us. We walked around to the back of the farm and I gasped when I saw the place.

Rustic wooden picnic benches had been set up in the field, all decorated with white ribbons. In the actual yard, wooden tables were loaded down with every kind of food imaginable. Everywhere I looked, white ribbons streamed and people milled around chatting and laughing. It was perfect.

The floral arrangements from the church had been brought along and each one was now a center piece for the tables with a small bundle of white and silver balloons floating above them. The barn and the house were strung with fairy lights, ready for when the sun went down.

Suzy elbowed me and pointed to the house. I followed her gaze. A huge white banner read, "Congratulations to the happy couple." At either end of it was a photo of Billy and me.

Autumn stood up as we approached the party. She had a megaphone and she didn't seem to be in the least bit uncomfortable about using it.

"Ladies and gentlemen, boys and girls," her voice boomed through it. "Please welcome the bride and groom."

I blushed once again as rapturous applause came from the gathered guests. I looked around, spotting all of the familiar faces. There was Margene Huffler, looking pretty in pink. Betty Blackwell was beside her, elegant in navy blue. Suzy's mom was sitting with my grandma and some of her reading group. I spotted Tucker at one of the tables with a pretty girl beside him hanging on his every word. It felt as though the whole town had turned out to greet us on our special day.

The most special guest, Snowball of course, ran towards me from behind the outhouse, which was also strung with fairy lights. She bleated happily, in her element with all of the people here who had no doubt all been giving her attention. Around her neck was a red bow which perfectly matched the color of the red roses in my bouquet and floral displays. I squatted down and petted Snowball, who gently nudged me with her nose as I scratched beneath her chin and then behind her ears.

She moved to Billy next and I laughed.

"She knows you're one of the family now," I said as he bent down to pat her.

Suzy had gone off in search of Emma Rose and Brian had followed behind her.

"Listen," I said to Billy while we were alone. "This dress doesn't exactly scream outdoorsy. I'm going to go inside and get changed. Can you keep people distracted for five minutes?"

"Of course," he agreed. He slipped his suit jacket off and held it out to me. "Can you take this with you? I kind of wish I'd brought my jeans, but this is a start."

I laughed and nodded, and then I headed towards the house. I hurried through the kitchen, pausing to hang Billy's jacket on the back of a chair, before I went to the attic stairs. It was only when I heard a familiar bleat as I put one foot on the bottom step that I realized Snowball had followed me inside. As she brushed past me on the way up the stairs, I wondered absently if she would smudge my dress, but then I noticed the smell of shampoo wafting up from her. I had to laugh at the thought of my grandma bathing her.

I hurried on up to my room, where I wriggled out of my dress and zipped it back into its bag. I loved my dress and wearing it had been like a dream come true. I had felt like a fairy tale princess in it. But at the same time, I would be glad to slip into something a little more comfortable. I kicked the high heels off, relieved they were gone and I could once more feel safe on my feet.

I had already laid my outfit out. A white dress that hit just above my knee. It was cotton and would keep me nice and cool. I had finally opted out of the spray tan to Suzy's dismay, but the white of this dress really brought out my natural tan. It had short sleeves and a panel of lace around the neckline. I slipped my feet into white ballet style shoes and laced the ribbons up my legs. I checked myself in the mirror. I looked fine, still bridal enough for anyone to know it was my wedding, thanks to the white, but comfortable enough to actually enjoy the party. It would be nice not to have to worry about breaking an ankle or ruining my dress.

I smiled to myself as I moved away from the mirror. Somehow, I had expected to look different now I was married, but of course I didn't. Well, except for my cheeks. They were glowing beneath my blush.

"Come on then girl, we've got a party to get to," I said to Snowball.

I made my way downstairs, followed by the little goat, and walked back towards the kitchen. My heart almost stopped as I stepped into the kitchen and saw a figure rushing towards me. I gasped and then laughed at my own nerves when I realized the figure was Betty Blackwell.

"Hi Betty. Is everything alright?" I asked.

She smiled at me. "That's what I was coming to ask you. I saw you slipping inside and thought maybe you were a little overwhelmed, but now I see what you were up to."

I was touched that she had noticed and made an effort to come and check on me.

"Oh, goodness me," she exclaimed before I had a chance to answer her.

Snowball had put her little hooves on Betty's legs and she was bleating incessantly.

"Snowball, stop it," I said.

She ignored me of course.

"She just wants to be fussed over," I said to Betty, moving closer to pick Snowball up.

Betty surprised me by bending down and laughing as she stroked the little goat.

"Aren't you just a friendly little thing?" she cooed as she stroked her.

I watched, fighting to hide my amusement at this softer side of Betty. Betty straightened back up and, satisfied, Snowball returned to my side.

"Congratulations, by the way," Betty said.

"Thank you," I replied.

"You know," she said as we walked out to the yard. "You didn't have to pay that wedding planner. I would have been more than happy to organize everything for you."

"That's really sweet, but I would never have asked that of you," I said. "I'm just happy you're here. Now no organizing today. Just relax and enjoy the party."

"I'll try." Betty smiled.

We crossed the yard and Suzy approached us.

"So now that you're finally here, we can eat, right?" She laughed.

"Right," I agreed.

"Good. I'll go talk to the caterer," she said.

"Allow me," Betty interrupted.

I laughed as Betty hurried away to harass the caterer. It was probably too much to ask for Betty to just relax and not take charge of something or someone. I didn't feel guilty. She would be in her element with a team of caterers to boss around.

"The caterer isn't going to know what hit her," Suzy joked.

"I know," I agreed.

I linked my arm through Suzy's and we made our way through the crowd to the head table. I kept stopping to greet people and chat with them, accepting compliments until I could feel my face reddening. We finally reached the table. I had barely touched down on the seat when Autumn shouted through her megaphone again.

"Ladies and gentlemen, the moment you have all been waiting for. The buffet is now open," she shouted with a laugh.

Her announcement was greeted with rapturous applause from the guests.

"What time is it?" I asked Billy.

"Stop worrying," he teased. "The band isn't due to start for another hour after the food and toasts are done. They're all set up and ready to go."

I grinned, amused that he had known exactly why I wanted to know.

"Come on, let's go eat. I don't know about you, but this wedding thing is making me hungry," Billy said.

I had to admit I was hungry. I had expected the nerves to overtake my hunger, but they most definitely hadn't. I reached the buffet table, surprised by the sheer amount of food there. It all looked so good it was hard to choose what to have. As I made my way along the table selecting tasty looking morsels, I spotted Tucker. I debated asking him how he was getting along on Summer's murder case, but I stopped myself. No, it was my wedding day. There was no way I was actively investigating a murder during my own reception.

We made our way back to the table. The conversation trailed off for the most part as everyone tucked into the food. The early morning start, which was unusual for most people although not for me and my grandparents, coupled with the fresh country air, certainly seemed to have given all of the guests a healthy appetite.

When we had finished eating, Autumn got her megaphone out again and asked for the speeches. My grandpa went first, giving a moving speech about how much he had always loved me, and how I was like a daughter to him. It was pretty much the most I had ever heard him say at one time and I felt myself tearing up more than once at his lovely words.

Suzy went next, expanding on her speech from the night before. Again, I felt myself tearing up as she talked. I looked around at the gathering. Hillbilly Hollow was more than just a town. It was a real community, an extended family who had opened their arms and welcomed back their prodigal daughter. I had never felt more loved, more accepted or more content than I did through Suzy's speech, as she talked about my return last year to Hillbilly Hollow and my once more filling the holes I had left in her heart, in Billy's heart, in my grand-parents' hearts and in the collective heart of the town.

Brian was up next, giving an uplifting, hilarious speech about Billy that was the perfect antidote to my tears. My eyes still felt wet, but this time it was with tears of laughter. Billy roared with laughter beside me.

"I'll get you back for this," Billy joked as Brian's speech finished to loud applause and he sat back down.

"Too late." Brian laughed, flashing his wedding ring at Billy.

Suzy stood back up.

"Now let's hear from the blushing bride and the lucky groom," she shouted.

More applause followed and I felt myself being pulled to my feet. I offered a quick thank you to everyone for coming, for welcoming me back, for the presents and cards and well wishes, and then I let Billy take over. He directed his speech at me, telling me how sad he had been when I'd left town, how happy he had been when I returned, and how he thought he had died and gone to heaven when I finally agreed to date him.

His speech was eloquent and full of raw emotion and by the time it was over, I had lost my battle with the tears and they flowed freely down my face. As I sat back down, I realized the moment was upon us for our first dance and I turned to Suzy in panic, knowing my mascara was streaked down my face and there would be pictures taken.

She quickly fixed my face, tears shining in her own eyes as she did it. The band subtly took to the makeshift stage. The lead singer spoke into the microphone.

"For the first time, please welcome to the floor Dr. and Mrs. Stone," he shouted.

Billy stood up and held out his hand to me. I smiled at him and took his hand and he led me out to the improvised dance floor, which consisted of floor tiles stuck onto a huge square of hardboard and laid down covering half of the field.

The band began to play a favorite song of ours. Billy pulled me into his arms and I rested my head on his shoulder as we held each other and moved in a slow circle to the music. The song was only a quarter of the way in when the guests began to clink their glasses, urging us to kiss.

"I think we'd better give the people what they want," Billy said.

"Yes, I'd hate to disappoint our guests," I agreed with a smile.

We kissed and as his lips touched mine, I felt a stirring deep inside me. That feeling told me I had definitely made the right decision. Billy had always been the one; it had just taken me far too long to see it.

We pulled back from the kiss and smiled lovingly at each other and then Billy shouted "come on", and beckoned and the dance floor was soon full of other couples. The band switched to something more lively and the party was well and truly underway, filled with laughter and dancing and a whole load of champagne.

We had made the slightly unconventional decision of

holding off on cutting the cake for awhile, letting people enjoy the party and have the first course settle first.

As I twirled and laughed on the dance floor, I had never been happier. This was exactly the wedding reception I'd always dreamed of, and I was married to the man of my dreams. What could be better than this?

10

I danced with Billy, and then with Suzy and then with my grandparents, each in turn. I danced with Betty Blackwell, who finally decided to let her hair down once she realized the catering staff were actually quite good at their jobs. I didn't know how long this more relaxed version of her could possibly last, but I knew I had to take my chance while it was there and have a little dance with her.

I danced with Beth and each of Billy's brothers and then I danced with Brian. When my feet were screaming at me and my throat was dry, I finally slipped off the dance floor, returned to our table and sat back down to take a long drink from my champagne. The bubbles fizzed down my nose and tears filled my eyes as it stung slightly. I shrugged. Worse things than that could have happened. I took another drink, being slightly more careful this time.

As I looked around at everyone having a good time, I had to admit that Autumn had done a superb job. Everything was great and running right on schedule. And Derrick was still in a more jovial mood than he had been yesterday, chatting and laughing with our guests.

Billy came over and reclaimed his seat by my side as I looked around, grinning happily. My cheeks ached from smiling, but I was so overwhelmingly happy that I just couldn't stop myself from doing it.

"I can't believe you dragged me out there to dance and then escaped yourself and left me there." He laughed.

"On the contrary, I believe it was you who dragged me up there," I retorted, joining in his laughter.

"All the same, it's nice to take a breather," he replied.

I nodded. It was. It was lovely to just sit back and take in the moment. People were still up dancing as the band belted out tune after tune. People sat at the various benches chatting, maybe catching up with friends they hadn't seen for awhile. All around us, the air was filled with love and laughter and magic. I wished I could take a mental picture of it all, because whatever happened in our futures, I never wanted to forget this moment.

"So, how does it feel to be my wife?" Billy asked.

"Perfect." I smiled. "I feel, I don't know, different somehow. Like we're official now."

The current song came to an end and the singer spoke into the microphone.

"Okay guys, we're going to take a short break now, but don't worry, we'll be back soon with more of your favorites. Don't go away."

The band left the stage to loud and heartfelt applause. There were whoops and cheers and even a loud whistle or two as well as the expected clapping of hands and stamping of feet. When the applause died down, Autumn's voice rang out through the megaphone again.

"Ladies and gentlemen, it's now time for the cutting of the cake. I'm sure you'll all join me in putting your hands together for Billy and Emma," she shouted.

I wasn't ready to move. My feet were still burning, but the guests were clapping and cheering and I didn't want to let anyone down. The cake looked delicious and I knew they were all eagerly waiting for a slice. I was very tempted by it myself.

Billy stood up and held his hand out to me. I slipped my hand into his and he pulled me to my feet. He didn't release his grip as we walked over to the cake table. Autumn beamed at us as we approached.

"Knock yourselves out, guys," she said, smiling.

She handed Billy a cordless microphone and faded away into the background, a skill I was sure she was much better at than Summer would have been. Billy made a short speech wherein he once again thanked everyone for coming.

Autumn pressed a large knife into my hand and, for just an instant, our fingers touched during the transfer. I didn't know why but a strange shudder passed through me during that second. There was something uncomfortable about holding such a wickedly sharp knife in front of a gathering that likely included a murderer. I didn't realize that I was staring wide-eyed at Autumn across from me until her own eyes narrowed. For just a moment, I imagined I could read in their blue depths some sort of malevolent emotion.

Then I felt Billy's light touch on my elbow. I broke eye contact with Autumn and the feeling passed.

I shook my strange thoughts away as Billy covered my small hand with his big one and we cut down into the cake. The guests went wild, clapping and cheering as we cut through the cake. I turned to Billy and smiled. He returned my smile and leaned down and kissed me as a hundred flashes went off, capturing our happiness.

We put the knife down and I looked around for Autumn, but she seemed suddenly to have disappeared. There was no sign of her anywhere. I sighed inwardly. The guests would expect to be served a slice of the cake pretty soon now. They were all moving back to their tables, waiting for the cake to be offered around, and I knew I would have to cut it all myself rather than keep them waiting.

I should have known it would never come to that. The thought was barely formed when Betty Blackwell was at my side.

"I don't know where that over-priced party organizer has rushed off to, but you listen to me, Emma. This is your wedding day, and you won't be doing this yourself. Now go and sit down and let me sort this out."

I opened my mouth to protest, but I was too late. Even as I had danced with Betty, I had known the more relaxed version of her wouldn't stay for long, and here she was proving me right. She was in her element when there was a job to be done, so I let her handle this for me.

"Beth. Suzy. Get on up here and help me," Betty shouted, turning away from me and going into organization mode.

Suzy raised an eyebrow as she made her way back up to the cake area and I shrugged. The conversation was easy for both of us to understand without words. Her asking what had happened to Autumn and me telling her I didn't know. She reached my side and gently pushed me and Billy away from the table.

"Go on. You heard Betty. Go and sit down and leave this to us," she said.

Suzy could give Betty a run for her money on who was the bossiest, and I allowed myself to be moved away from the table. I had no chance of having my protests heard now that Suzy and Betty had joined forces against me, even if I still wanted to protest, which I really didn't. Surely everyone deserved a little break on their own wedding day.

Billy and I went back to our table and sat down. I scanned the field and the yard, trying to spot Autumn. She must have gone to the outhouse, I thought to myself. I spotted my grandma and grandpa talking to Margene Huffler. Snowball was by their side and Margene seemed quite taken with her.

I looked away, and that was when I saw her. Not Autumn, but Summer. She stood off to one side of the festivities, an ethereal figure in the distance. No one else noticed her, of course, since they didn't share my gift for seeing the dead. For all I couldn't see her closely enough to know exactly where she was looking, I knew just the same. She was looking at me. I could feel her eyes boring into me and a shiver ran through my body.

"Are you alright?" Billy asked with concern in his voice.

I forced out a laugh. "I'm fine," I reassured him. "I just got a bit of a shiver there. A goose must have walked over my grave."

I looked back to the spot where Summer had been, but she was already gone. Why had she come here today? Was she trying to give me a message? Was she telling me to watch Derrick more closely, or was she telling me I was right with my suspicions about Doris? Or maybe I was focusing on the wrong people...

Suddenly, it hit me, although I couldn't have said where the knowledge came from. Autumn was the one who had disappeared and it was Autumn Summer was trying to warn me about. As the pieces fell into place in my head, I didn't know how I hadn't seen it sooner. I had suspected Autumn for a time, but it was a short time and I had written her off as a suspect pretty much straight away. But it was all there, I just hadn't been looking for it. Not really.

I'd had two perfectly likely suspects and I'd stuck with them. But of course, both of those suspects had been handed to me on a plate by Autumn, one way or the other. How had I not noticed that the evidence I had managed to gather so far all centered around her? It didn't matter now, it only mattered that I had finally put everything together.

It had been Autumn who had put the idea of Derrick as a suspect into my mind, painting him to be someone threatening with a grudge against Summer. Clearly she had been planning this murder for quite some time and she had already begun planting seeds of suspicion before she did the dirty deed.

It had been Autumn who had led me to the threatening notes in Summer's desk. In an office she conveniently mentioned not being able to face entering. A chance for her to have plausible deniability for the notes.

Summer was far too organized not to keep all of her client's files in her office. And now that I knew, I could see her office in my mind. I could see the empty shelf amongst the books, an anomaly uncharacteristic of Summer. It must be the place Autumn had cleared when she moved the files to a common area in case I checked her story. Or in case Tucker went there.

But she had known he wouldn't. By her own admission, she knew he was no detective. But she had obviously known who I was. She had clearly known I would go poking around, and she had carefully executed a plan to give me, not one, but two suspects and keep my suspicions firmly away from her.

If it wasn't for the fact that I now believed she had murdered her sister, I would find myself grudgingly admiring her for the simplicity of the plan she had used to throw me off the scent.

Now that I had seen it, though, there was no unseeing it. It made so much sense. It made it clear why she was okay when she caught me snooping around her building, why she was so quick to allow me access to Summer's office. She had planted the notes and she had wanted me to find them. Catching me in the act and being annoyed about it had all been part of her act.

It also explained why she didn't push me to tell her what I had found in Summer's office. I had put it down to shock at losing her sister, to grief. But it hadn't been. She didn't want to start asking questions and risk tripping herself up. And she had known exactly what I had found anyway, without having to risk asking the wrong question or saying the wrong thing. She must have somehow stolen a notepad from Doris's shop and written those notes herself.

The more I let myself go down that path, the better I could see it. The notes that were supposedly from Doris had been written on notepaper with her current header. But that wouldn't have been right. She wouldn't have waited so long after Summer had ripped her off to start sending threatening notes, if that was what she had wanted to do. The ripping off of Doris had happened long before Flower Power was rebranded. I knew this for a fact because I had done the design work for Doris. If Doris had genuinely sent those notes, it would have been on paper headed with her old logo.

Autumn wouldn't have known that I had worked on Flower Power's rebranding. She couldn't have known that I would know the exact date the logo changed and would work out from that knowledge that the notes had to be faked.

My mind was whirling, churning it all over. Was it possible that Autumn had somehow sensed I was getting close to the truth? Had I unconsciously betrayed with a word or look the suspicion that even I hadn't known was growing at the back of my mind?

Those were all questions I still couldn't answer yet, but I knew I had answered the most important one: who had killed Summer Martin.

Autumn had by far the most to gain from the death of

her sister. She got full ownership of a business she had put her heart and soul into but still owned less than half of. She got to do things her way, by building genuine relationships with her vendors rather than making enemies of them. She got her nagging older sister off her back.

"Here you go, honey," Suzy said, putting a plate in front of me with a slice of my wedding cake on it. She frowned slightly when she saw the expression on my face. "Emma? Are you alright? You look like you've seen a ghost."

Oh, if she only knew.

"I'm fine." I laughed. "Honestly, everyone keeps asking me if I'm alright and I swear I'm starting to get a complex over it. I'm just looking around, trying to take it all in."

Suzy frowned. She didn't push me to say any more, but I could see by her determined expression she would be trying to corner me later to find out what was wrong with me. Hopefully by then this would be dealt with and I could tell her.

I wanted to jump up and try to sort this whole mess out right now, but I knew it would be seen as rude not to partake in a piece of my own wedding cake. And Billy and I had only been married for a couple of hours. He didn't deserve to have me running out on him before we'd even shared our wedding cake.

I picked up my piece of the dessert and nibbled the edge of it. The orange flavored sponge cake with a beautiful dark chocolate ganache melted in my mouth.

"From now on, you're in charge of choosing every

cake we ever eat," Billy said as he swallowed his first bite. "This is delicious."

"You should thank the baker for that." I laughed. "I had the easy job of just tasting it, remember?"

"Well, you have good taste," he said.

"Does she?" a voice asked. "Because she married you, didn't she?"

I laughed as I looked up at Billy's brother. He plonked himself down next to Billy and started chatting with him. I tried to eat my cake quickly but not quickly enough to look suspicious. This would be my perfect opportunity to slip away while I wasn't leaving Billy sitting here alone.

I was a little upset at not having time to savour every bite of the gorgeous cake, but I knew there would be enough left over to last a long time to come, and I also knew it was much more important to deal with an actual murderer running loose at my wedding than it was to finish the piece of cake slowly.

I finally finished the last bite and stood up.

"Would you excuse me for a moment?" I smiled. "I've just spotted someone I've been dying to catch up with."

Billy nodded, barely looking up from his conversation with his brother, which was a good thing as I cringed when I realized I had used the word dying. One look at that expression on my face would have had him watching me to see who I was going to talk to and to make sure I was okay.

I moved away from our table quickly, before Billy could ask me anything about who I wanted to see. I had barely covered five steps when my grandma and Margene Huffler waved me over to their table. I couldn't very well pretend I hadn't seen them. They weren't stupid. And if my grandma got even the slightest inkling that I was doing anything except enjoying my wedding reception, she would be so angry. Probably even angrier than Billy would be if he found out. The decision made for me, I went over to their table.

"Are you enjoying yourself, dear? You look a little lost," Grandma said.

I noticed Snowball sitting beneath their table being fed treats from both of them and from my Grandpa, who was deep in conversation with a couple of his farming buddies but who kept looking away long enough to hold out a tasty morsel or two to Snowball.

"I was just wandering around, taking in the atmosphere and doing a bit of people watching," I lied.

"That's so much fun, isn't it?" Margene said. "It's surely one of the best things about parties. That and the scandals and gossip you hear."

My grandma frowned and Margene rushed on.

"Not here, of course. Dorothy has made it very clear that's not what today is about. I know that, of course, I just meant in general. And by the way, I didn't get a chance to tell you how stunning you looked in your dress."

"Thank you," I beamed, not really sure if I was thanking her for the compliment about my dress or for the promise that she wouldn't turn my wedding into next week's hot gossip topic.

"Are you both enjoying yourselves?" I asked.

Margene nodded. "Oh yes, dear," she said.

My grandma finished up the last bite of her slice of wedding cake and grinned at me.

"How could we not be enjoying ourselves when there's cake this delicious?" she said.

I leaned in closer and whispered to her and Margene, "There's plenty left. Go on up and get yourself some more."

They didn't need telling twice, and I was once more free to roam around trying to spot Autumn. I couldn't see her anywhere. Suddenly, I felt myself getting angry. This was my wedding day. I shouldn't be spending it chasing down a murderer. Not for Summer, not for anyone.

I made my decision. I was in no mood to confront a killer. Not here. Not today. Instead, for once, I was going to have to put my faith in Tucker. I would give him all of the information he needed, and let him chase Autumn down and get a confession out of her. That might not solve the case quickly and efficiently, but it would surely pacify Summer's ghost if she saw me talking to the sheriff and giving him everything he needed to see justice done.

I nodded to myself, my decision made. I looked around the crowd again, this time searching for Tucker. I felt a deep sense of frustration when I realized I couldn't spot him either. What was with this day? People were meant to be gathered in one place and they should be around when I needed them.

I told myself to stop being such a brat. It was not as though Tucker even knew I was looking into Summer's murder, let alone that I had solved it and needed to find him to tell him about it. I kept looking, weaving between the tables, constantly getting stopped by guests wanting to say hello or ask me if I was having a good time, or one of a million other small questions. I tried my best to answer each person with a genuine smile, a genuine response, and not to look like I was trying to just move away from them. I reminded myself they had all turned out here today for Billy and me and the least they deserved was a smile and a few words.

I still hadn't spotted Tucker or the pretty blonde he was with earlier when I reached the far side of the field. I did, however, spot Betty Blackwell. If anyone knew where Tucker was it would be her.

"Betty." I smiled as I walked up to her. "Thank you so much for organizing the cake slicing."

She smiled back at me. "What are friends for, Emma? It was no trouble at all. It made me feel useful."

I said, "You're always useful Betty. There's nothing you won't do for this community."

She waved my praise away, blushing slightly.

"You haven't seen Sheriff Tucker, have you?" I asked, trying to make it sound casual.

"Is something wrong?" Betty asked, instantly suspicious.

I shook my head, giving her what I hoped was a genuine looking smile.

"No, not at all. I just wanted to ask him to keep an eye on the farm while Billy and I are on our honeymoon. Not that I think anything will happen or that my grandparents aren't more than capable of taking care of themselves. It'll just give me peace of mind, that's all."

"Oh, you're such a sweetheart." Betty smiled.

I wasn't entirely sweet as I was standing here lying to

her face, but if she got wind of what I really wanted, I could imagine her organizing a man hunt for Autumn and I wasn't about to risk her or anyone else getting hurt.

And it wasn't a total lie. I did want peace of mind while Billy and I were away. Betty didn't need to know I had already called Tucker yesterday and had that conversation with him.

"I'm only doing what anyone would," I said.

"I'm not sure about that, Emma. Not everyone cares enough to do something like that, you know. You should give yourself a little more credit."

I smiled and felt myself blushing at her words.

"So? Have you seen him?" I asked, not able to think of a more subtle way to drive the conversation back to my original question.

"Yes, in fact I have," she said, frowning. "He went for a walk and headed off in that direction." She stopped and pointed out through the next field. "With that blonde girl," she added meaningfully.

I couldn't help but laugh. "Well, I'll try and catch up to them."

There was no question of postponing my conversation with Tucker. This was too important.

I managed to slip away without being stopped again, which wasn't a huge surprise as the field I had to cross wasn't really part of the party.

When I rounded the screen of a few trees along the fence line it quickly became obvious that Tucker and his companion were nowhere in sight. I peeked around the far side of the barn and, again, there was no sign of them. Looking up at the old barn itself looming over me, I decided to duck my head in the door just to make sure they hadn't gone inside.

I slid the barn door open a crack and stepped in. I heard footsteps to my right and turned in that direction, opening my mouth to speak. But my mouth went dry and my heart started racing as I found myself looking, not at Tucker, but straight at Autumn Martin.

11

I stood frozen to the spot for a moment as Autumn and I stared at each other. I wondered if maybe there was an easy way out of this. There was at least a chance that Autumn still had no idea that I knew her secret. It was unlikely but I had to test the theory. Even if she suspected I knew, I could perhaps convince her otherwise.

"Are you alright?" I asked, trying to sound as normal as I could, concerned even. "It's just that I noticed you were missing and I wanted to make sure everything was okay."

As I spoke, Autumn moved slightly, circling me without taking her eyes off me. She moved to stand in front of the barn door, and even before she spoke, I knew that she knew I'd put the pieces of the puzzle together. Why else would she try to block my escape route?

I could still wangle out of this by feigning ignorance, though. If I could convince her I didn't know anything, surely she wouldn't push it in case she inadvertently confessed everything to someone who didn't actually know what was going on.

"You can drop the act, Emma," she replied.

Her tone was resigned, quiet. Not venomous or angry. I had to try and respond how I would if I knew nothing and was really here because Autumn had bailed on me.

"Fine," I replied. "I don't really care if you're alright. I'm paying you a lot of money to make sure my wedding reception goes off smoothly and you disappeared when the cake needed cutting. What's going on?"

Autumn laughed sadly. "If I didn't know better, you could have almost had me fooled there. You should think about taking up a job as an actress," she said.

"I don't understand what you mean," I said.

"Quit it," Autumn snapped. "We both know you've figured me out. I saw the knowledge in your eyes when I handed you the knife to cut the cake. In that second, you realized the truth."

I didn't correct her or explain that it was only a funny feeling I'd had during the cake cutting. The actual revelation hadn't come until a few minutes later. Still, there was no point in playing dumb either. Autumn clearly knew I'd worked it all out, and I figured my best course of action was to keep her talking. Billy would notice I was missing eventually, and Betty would remember sending me toward the barn. They would find me in time to stop Autumn from harming me. I had to cling to that hope.

"Why did you do it?" I asked.

"Why do you think?" Autumn asked, rolling her eyes. "You heard the way Summer talked to me. I couldn't take it anymore. I snapped."

"Now who's playing games?" I asked. "You didn't snap. You planned it. That's why you were feeding me lines about Derrick the photographer and stirring up suspicions about Doris the florist, so I could pass that information on to Tucker and give you a few potential suspects."

"Oh, whatever. I might as well tell you," Autumn said.

She tried to make herself sound bored as she said it, but I could see she was dying to tell someone how clever she had been. I could use that knowledge to draw the conversation out and make it last.

"Maybe it will do me good to get it all off my chest," she went on. "You're right. I did plan it. Summer was getting worse, treating me more horribly by the day. And it didn't hurt that I knew if I got her out of the way without being blamed for her murder, that I would get full ownership of the business. But Derrick was a happy accident. I honestly wasn't trying to make you suspect him when we talked about him. It was just chatter. I had already decided to frame Doris Young for the killing. I'm sure you know her motive. That Summer ripped her off on a deal?"

I nodded. Again Autumn had surprised me with her revelation about Derrick and how he was never meant to be a suspect.

"Doris was rightfully angry at Summer. Even I was angry with her when I found out what had happened. But Doris never did believe me when I told her that I wasn't involved in the deception and she blamed me equally for it all, even though I wasn't involved. I was dating a lovely man, my soul mate, but he knew Doris and Doris told him what happened and implicated me.

He ended our relationship. So who better to frame for Summer's murder than Doris, right? It meant I could get revenge on two people who had wronged me."

I was curious and I found myself itching to ask Autumn some questions. She must have seen that in my face.

"Come on, out with it. It's obvious you have questions. You might as well ask them," she said.

"Why did you hide the notes in Summer's office? You knew Sheriff Tucker wouldn't look there," I said.

"But you would. I knew you wouldn't be able to keep your perfect little nose out of it."

I raised an eyebrow and Autumn laughed.

"You have quite the reputation in this town, Emma, if you know who to ask. Detective extraordinaire and all that. For what it's worth, I'm genuinely sorry this had to happen right on top of your wedding, but I had everything in hand. I had been paying very close attention to all of your wedding prep and knew I could step in and take over. Which I did, right?"

"Right," I agreed, unsure what else to say.

"I had no intentions of bailing on you today, but then I saw during the cake cutting how the wheels were turning in your mind as you put it all together. If you hadn't felt the need to poke your nose in, I would have gotten away with it. And you wouldn't have had to deal with your own cake."

"I had to 'poke my nose in,' as you so delicately put it. Somebody had to see that justice was done."

She looked up at me, a puzzled expression on her face. "I just have one question," she said.

I nodded. If it would keep her talking, I would answer anything she asked me.

"What gave me away? I covered my tracks perfectly. How did you know?"

I thought about it for a moment.

"It was a lot of little things. You didn't seem particularly upset at Summer's death, but at first I put that down to shock and grief. The same with how you had very little interest in what I'd found in Summer's office. See, I thought you didn't want to know because you were hurting. I thought of how I would have reacted in your situation, and my first thought was that I would have gone absolutely crazy asking you questions. But then I decided maybe I wouldn't have. Maybe I would have been too upset to want to hear all of the sordid details. Of course you had a solid motive for murdering Summer. But again, I dismissed that because Doris looked to be a much better suspect after I found the notes. Well played."

Autumn smiled and shrugged like it was nothing. Like she planned murders all the time. Maybe the wedding planning had made her more aware of catching every little detail. Or maybe murder was her speciality. Who knew?

I continued, "All through the investigation, I could feel something niggling at the back of my mind, a clue I had missed. And then, around the time I realized you had gone missing from the reception, it all began to come together. But I guess that was just a lucky coincidence."

"So I turned out to be your niggling doubt?" Autumn asked.

I nodded.

"That makes sense, I suppose. But it doesn't really answer my question. What convinced you that you were right about me? You said you had dismissed the suspicions. What finally made you see that I wasn't in shock, only pretending to be?"

"The notepaper you used to forge Doris's threatening notes on," I admitted. "The note paper had her new logo on it. Summer ripped her off a long time ago, so it should have been on the old note paper from before her rebrand."

Autumn narrowed her eyes. "You're lying to me," she said. "There's no way you could know the exact date of her rebrand. I considered every aspect of this murder and even I didn't know that much."

"But you're not the graphic designer who redesigned her logo, are you?" I asked.

Autumn threw her head back and laughed. "And you are? Wow. You really couldn't make this up, could you? I had everything covered down to the tiniest detail, and something completely out of my control, something that no one would ever consider, is what tipped you off?"

I nodded. "Yeah. Pretty much."

"So maybe you're not quite the detective you think you are. Maybe you just got lucky," Autumn said.

Her words angered me. Who was she to stand there doubting my skills at anything? I had proved time and again that I was a pretty good detective. And if a bit of luck was involved, then so be it.

"Maybe I did, but I still got to the right answer, didn't I?" I reminded her.

She conceded the point. "You did. And I guess rather

than saying you got lucky, we would be more accurate in saying you got unlucky."

"How's that?" I asked.

She smiled, a cold smile that sent a shiver down my spine.

"Because now I'll have to kill you too," she said, like this should have been obvious to me. In some ways, it was. I had known it would come to this. "You know too much. You are literally the only thing standing between me and my freedom."

The same was true of her. With her body still blocking the barn door, she was standing between me and my freedom every bit as much as I was standing between her and hers.

"You'll never get away with killing me," I said. "You haven't planned on this."

"Really? Because you said it yourself. Sheriff Tucker is hardly the best detective, is he? He will have no real chance of solving this without you around."

My heart sank. She was most likely right about that one.

"But just to be clear, you're wrong. I do have a plan for this one too. Don't you worry about that. I had to have a plan in case you got too close to the truth. When I disappeared when it was time for you to cut the cake, I didn't come away empty handed."

With a movement of her wrist, she revealed for the first time something she had been hiding behind her back—a sharp-looking knife that was identical to the one I had cut my wedding cake with. There hadn't been time for her to snatch the real cake-cutting knife from the table, not underneath everybody's noses, so I knew this one must be only an extra from the same set. But the fact that it was decorative made it no less sharp and deadly.

Autumn continued to speak. "Sheriff Tucker coming across this way with his date gave me the last part of my idea. I knew you would search for him—the look on your face back at the cake table left me in no doubt you'd take action soon – so I sneaked out here, knowing it was only a matter of time until someone told you he had come toward the barn."

"What did you do to him?" I demanded, eying the knife held so casually in her hand.

Autumn waved my concern away. "I didn't do anything to either Sheriff Tucker or his little blonde date. They never did come into the barn. They kept walking. But I knew you would check in here. I just had to bide my time and hope you came looking for him, which you did."

"So, what now?" I asked.

"I'm going to kill you and then sneak back to the party. I'm going to hunt down Sheriff Tucker and tell him how worried I am about you. I'll tell him all about how you were investigating Summer's death and how you found some threatening notes from Doris Young, which you passed on to me. Don't worry, I have plenty more where those first few came from, so if anyone finds the ones you had after your death, they'll just assume you hung on to some of them for whatever reason. Probably because you're so nosey."

"Tucker won't believe your story," I said, although I was very much afraid he might.

She ignored me and continued talking. "I'll tell the

sheriff how you swore me to secrecy, saying you needed to find more evidence before you came to him because if Doris got wind of the fact she was a suspect, she might be able to wriggle out of the charges. Tucker won't know the exact date Doris's branding changed. When she tells him about it, he won't believe her. It'll sound like the desperate excuses of a woman caught out. He might even go so far as to assume the rebrand was to try and hide what she had done, although that might be a little bit too sophisticated for him to think up on his own. And the only person who could corroborate Doris's claims about that date, you, will be dead."

She clucked her tongue in mock sadness. "Such a tragedy. I'll tell the sheriff I hate to break your confidence, but I saw Doris skulking around the party, and when I looked for you to warn you, I couldn't find you. I'll play it so I'm worried enough to spur him into action. Your body will be found and Doris will go down for a double murder."

Watching the way Autumn's fist tightened around the handle of the knife as she spoke, I thought desperately, trying to find a way out of this one.

"What if Doris has an alibi? She could be with people who can tell the sheriff where she was at the time of my murder," I said.

I didn't much like the sound of that. My murder.

Autumn shrugged. "There will be a point in time where she was alone. The coroner will only be able to give an approximate window for your time of death, and Flower Power closes at noon on a Saturday, so there's bound to be a space where Doris was alone. If it doesn't match exactly with the coroner's estimates, well, people will say it's not an exact science. It must have been a little off. There won't be any other suspects and the case will be closed and I'll once more be free."

As much as I hated to admit it, she was right about pretty much all of it. That was exactly how it would go down.

I swallowed hard as Autumn eyed me. Her body became taut and I knew she was getting ready to attack me. The time for talking her out of this had passed. Now it was time to fight for my life.

Autumn ran at me, the knife in her hand raised. Unthinkingly, I reacted. One moment I was standing there, helpless and unarmed. The next, I had snatched up a shovel lying near my feet. Grandpa must have forgotten to put it away after his morning chores. I was grateful he hadn't been his usually tidy self for once.

I swung out wildly with my awkward weapon, the shovel head striking Autumn in the wrist. She let out a pained cry and there was a clanging sound as the shovel met the metal of the knife. With a flash of silver, the knife spun through the air and landed several yards away. Unfortunately, I had lost my grip on the shovel handle during my clumsy swing and now the tool sailed out of my hands and across the barn to land in the dust. It was farther away than the knife, too far away to recover.

To my surprise, the injury to her hand hardly slowed Autumn down. She flew at me across the distance, bare-handed now. I raised my own hands, deflecting a punch that Autumn aimed at my throat. My deflection only seemed to anger her further. She roared again, and this time, she didn't try to punch me. She grabbed my throat and began to squeeze it, throttling me. I couldn't breathe and I could feel myself starting to panic as I clawed desperately at her hands, trying to get them off me. She clung on for dear life.

I kicked out blindly, landing a lucky shot on Autumn's shin. She screeched in pain and anger and for a second, her grip relaxed. I took my chance and wrenched my neck from her grip, grimacing at the stinging pain in the skin there from the friction of her hands. As I pulled my neck free, I shoved Autumn square in the chest and she stumbled backwards.

Her arms pinwheeled frantically as she fought to keep her balance. It was a fight she lost and she fell to the ground with an "oomph" sound. I hoped she would stay down long enough for me to get the upper hand, but she bounced straight back up again, fire in her eyes.

Worse, her hands were no longer empty. While she had been on the ground, she had located her sharp knife again.

We stood facing off against each other, panting, each waiting for the right moment to strike. I looked around frantically for something I could use as a weapon to defend myself. There was nothing close enough to be useful, so my eyes were drawn to the barn door. Autumn had moved away from it as we circled each other. I was confident I could outrun her. I just had to get to the door and run back to the party, screaming at the top of my lungs.

I turned and sprinted for the door. I heard Autumn's gasp of surprise, heard her feet running behind me. She was surprisingly fast and as I reached out for the door, seconds from freedom, I felt her hand clamp down on my shoulder.

Autumn spun me to face her. Her fist clutching the silver knife rose in the air, prepared to strike down at my heart. But just then, I saw a flash of white behind her shoulder. For a second I thought it was Molly, but then I realized I could hear the barn owl hooting in alarm from somewhere much deeper in the barn. The flash of white flew to the ceiling, and as Autumn's knife lowered toward me, a large rafter fell from above.

As I heard the rafter tearing loose, I knew without any doubt what that flash of white had been. The ghost of Summer Martin was protecting me from her murderous sister.

"Thank you, Summer," I whispered.

A flash of white light in the corner of the barn told me she had heard my thanks, but there was no more time to think of Summer.

I turned my attention back to Autumn, to the rafter that was falling, seemingly in slow motion, towards her. She had raised her head slightly and dropped her knife, seeming frozen to the spot. She could see the rafter coming, but she was too late to do anything to stop it or even to move out of its path.

It struck Autumn's head with a sickening cracking sound, narrowly missing me as I jumped backward instinctively.

Autumn's knees buckled and she crumpled to the ground. Her eyes closed and a trickle of blood ran from her forehead.

My heart was racing. I threw myself on the ground beside her and dragged the rafter off of her. I pushed two fingers against the side of her neck, feeling for a pulse. Relief flooded me when I found a strong, steady pulse in her throat. She was just unconscious.

I could make my escape now. I stood back up, but as I headed for the door, it sprang open. Tucker and Betty Blackwell stood in the doorway. Their eyes went from me to the unconscious Autumn and back again.

"I told you that Autumn girl was bad news," Betty said triumphantly.

"Looks to me like Autumn is the one injured," Tucker said gravely, moving to kneel beside the woman on the ground.

"You know as well as I do that Emma wouldn't have hurt that girl unprovoked," Betty scoffed. "Tell him, Emma."

"Actually, I didn't hurt her at all. A rafter fell from the roof and hit her," I explained.

"See. I told you," Betty said.

"She was trying to kill me at the time, though," I added. "With that knife."

I pointed to where the knife that had nearly ended my life glittered on the dusty ground nearby.

Tucker's eyes widened in shock. "Maybe you can explain while we wait for an ambulance," he said. "It doesn't look like the knock on her head was too bad, but we'd best be on the safe side."

I waited while he pulled out his cell and called the nearest hospital.

When he got off the phone I said, "I'll tell you every-thing, but before I do, what are you two even doing here?"

"You seemed to have been gone awhile and I was concerned about you," Betty said. "So I came to look for you. I didn't anticipate something like this, though. I thought maybe you'd fallen or something."

"And I was on my way back to the party. My date got a call to go in to work and I walked her to her car. She couldn't get parked out front so she was on the road that runs down the side of the farm. I took a shortcut," Tucker said.

That explained where he was heading and why he had cut across the field.

I spent the next couple of minutes hastily telling Tucker everything that had happened and everything I had found out since Summer's death. Well, everything except my ghostly visitor's appearances. When I had finished, Tucker sighed.

"I'm not saying I don't believe you, Emma. I do believe you. You know that, right?"

I nodded, waiting for him to go on.

"But the notes alone aren't evidence that Autumn set Doris up. They're evidence that Doris was set up, but there's no proof Autumn is the one who wrote them. It could have been anyone who knew enough to wait until Autumn was out of the office before sneaking in and planting the notes.

"I know you said she admitted everything to you, but she's unlikely to confess it on the record. And it looks like she came out of your fight a lot worse than you did, so I can't even hold her for assault."

"Then what happens now? She just gets away with it?" I asked.

"Of course not," Tucker replied. "I'll find the evidence. It just might take awhile."

I sat down heavily on a hay bale. Autumn had pulled off her crime perfectly. There wouldn't be any evidence; she was smarter than that. She could claim the knife she had attacked me with had been brought into the barn by me, and it would only be my word against hers. And she wasn't going to have whatever tool she'd used to cut Summer's brakes lying around her house with brake fluid on it. She might have the rest of Doris's notepad, but she would have the sense to destroy it as soon as she was home from the hospital. Tucker wouldn't be able to search her property without a warrant, and by the time he got one, it would be too late.

Just then, Autumn moaned from the ground, ending our discussion. She sat up slowly, her hand going to her head.

"What happened?" she asked groggily.

"A loose rafter fell from the roof and caught your head," Tucker said, moving back to her side. "If you feel like you can walk, I'm going to get you out to the front driveway. The ambulance should be pulling up any minute to take you to the hospital so they can check you over for a concussion."

Autumn ignored that last bit of information. "Why are you all looking at me that way? Emma has been talking, hasn't she? Even after I almost killed her, she has to have her ugly little nose in, doesn't she? Well, let me tell you something. It's her word against mine. And there is absolutely no proof that I faked those notes or that I murdered Summer."

"Actually, I beg to differ," Tucker said, standing up. "Your confession in front of witnesses aside, I have an idea that knife on the floor is going to be covered in your fingerprints and no one else's."

Autumn began to struggle in Tucker's grip then, but he cuffed her easily. I guessed it was a lucky thing he was in uniform and prepared for anything, even at a wedding reception. He pulled out his cell phone again.

"This is Sheriff Tucker out in the barn on the Hooper farm. I need urgent back up. I have a murderer on my hands."

Within minutes, several deputies appeared. They dragged Autumn away kicking and shouting. I had an idea that ambulance Tucker had called wasn't going to be needed. She certainly seemed to have got her strength back now.

"I'll get you for this, Emma. And you, old lady, you had better watch your back too."

"I am an old lady," Betty said. "And a lady is more than could ever be said for you."

She turned to me, while Autumn's threats faded into the background as she was dragged away.

"Come on, honey. Let's go back to the party. Don't let this ruin the most special day of your life. Her words and behaviour have proved her guilt to anyone who may have doubted it. The sheriff never did, and for what it's worth, neither did I."

I smiled at Betty as we began to walk back to the reception.

"Thank you," I said. "And you were right earlier. I never should have hired a wedding planner. You would have been the far superior choice."

"And you wouldn't have had to worry about any of your guests getting murdered either. Maybe worked to death, but not murdered."

It felt strange to be laughing so soon after I was nearly killed, but it felt good too. Betty and I were still laughing as we rejoined the party, to be met by an anxious Billy.

"What's going on? I saw Tucker and a lot of other cops coming from the barn," he said.

"It's a long story. Why don't you grab Betty and I a drink and a big slice of our cake, and I'll explain everything," I said.

12

T he party was still going at full swing at nine o'clock when it was time for Billy and I to leave for the airport, and I had a feeling it would still be going for a good few hours after we left. The band was playing and everyone was back to having fun, the misadventure of earlier forgotten, for the most part.

Those closest to me had been told what happened, but the rest of the guests were simply told that there had been an accident in the barn but everyone was fine now. The rest they would learn in the next morning's paper. Or more likely from my grandma and Margene Huffler after Billy and I left for the night. I was sure Betty would keep them in check and not let the story get too out of hand.

I'd told Billy everything, and he had been more relieved that I was safe than mad that I was investigating a murder through our wedding. He had just shook his head and made a comment about how I was unpredictable but he loved me just the same.

My grandparents had been informed of the damage

in the barn and I had taken my grandma aside and told her the truth about the rafter, including the part about Summer's ghost. She and Billy were the only ones I told about that. Grandma would tell Grandpa and he would be the only one she would tell; she was a gossip, but not when it came to anything associated with our family. Billy insisted he would pay for the repairs to the barn, but my grandparents wouldn't hear of it.

Tucker had come back to the party at that point. He told us that Autumn had been released from the hospital with no concussion and she had been officially charged with Summer's murder and my attempted murder and had made a full confession.

I felt a little guilty for suspecting Doris for so long, but Autumn was clever and she had led me expertly down a path that had felt like the only one at that time. I didn't think Doris would ever find out that she had been a suspect of mine, and if she ever did, I just had to hope she would understand why.

I had told Suzy a version of the truth; a version that didn't include ghosts or investigations. Just that I had stumbled across Autumn and she had snapped, confessing to killing her sister and then trying to kill me too. Suzy had been shocked and had pulled me into a tight hug.

As she hugged me, she whispered in my ear. "I know there's more to this, but I'm not going to press you for it. Just know that when you're ready to tell me, I'm ready to listen and I won't judge you."

She had then held me out at arm's length and, with tears in her eyes, told me that marriage suited me.

Billy and I made our way around all of the guests, thanking them for coming and hugging them all good-bye. Finally, I got to my grandparents and hugged them each in turn. Billy had just taken my hand in his and started forward a step when I heard a bleat from behind me. I gasped. Snowball. How could I have forgotten her?

I dropped Billy's hand and crouched down in front of Snowball. I scratched her chin and behind her ears and she bleated softly, rubbing her head against my knees. It was almost as though she knew I would be away for awhile, and that even once I returned, everything would have changed.

"Emma? We really do need to leave if we're to stand any chance of catching our flight," Billy said.

I planted a kiss on the top of Snowball's head and stood up. I gave each of my grandparents another quick hug and we walked to the car, the guests following behind us. The luggage was already loaded in the trunk and we got into the car, Billy holding my door open and closing it behind me once I was seated. He went around to get in beside me and quickly doubled checked the glove compartment, making sure we had our passports and tickets. When he was sure everything was in place, he turned to me and smiled.

"Well, we really did it," he said.

"We really did." I smiled back.

Our guests lined the driveway. As Billy drove down the road, they threw birdseed at the car, waving and shouting for us to have a good time. I waved back and blew kisses. I watched them in the rearview mirror as they shrunk and then they were finally out of sight.

As we drove to the airport, I found myself focusing on our honeymoon. It was going to be so fun and relaxing. After the whole Summer thing, it was exactly what I needed: a few weeks with no ghosts and no drama. Just me and Billy soaking up the sun and enjoying each other's company.

The ghosts and the investigating and danger could get exhausting at times, but even though I was looking forward to a break from it all, I knew I wouldn't change a thing about my life now.

While we were gone, I would miss this town and its assortment of characters, particularly my grandparents, Suzy and Brian and little Emma Rose. And of course Snowball. And although I was filled with excitement for this new adventure, excited to see a new part of the world with Billy beside me, I knew that when the time came to come back home, I would be excited about that too. For all of its eccentricities and the way trouble somehow seemed to search me out here, Hillbilly Hollow would always be my home. That was just how it was meant to be.

~

Margene Huffler's daughter has left Hillbilly Hollow! Follow Prudence Marianne as she moves across the country to delve into the magical mysteries of a small Colorado town in "A Sinister Spell in Faerywood Falls."

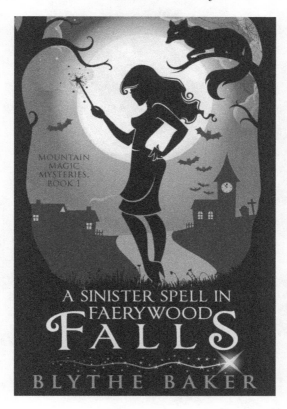

MOUNTAIN
MAGIC
MYSTERIES,
BOOK 1

A SINISTER SPELL IN
FAERYWOOD
FALLS

BLYTHE BAKER

ABOUT THE AUTHOR

Blythe Baker is a thirty-something bottle redhead from the South Central part of the country. When she's not slinging words and creating new worlds and characters, she's acting as chauffeur to her children and head groomer to her household of beloved pets.

Blythe enjoys long walks with her dog on sweaty days, grubbing in her flower garden, cooking, and ruthlessly de-cluttering her overcrowded home. She also likes binge-watching mystery shows on TV and burying herself in books about murder.

To learn more about Blythe, visit her website and sign up for her newsletter at www.blythebaker.com

CPSIA information can be obtained
at www.ICGtesting.com
Printed in the USA
BVHW030249080520
579407BV00001B/48